Praise for

THE SIMON B. RHYMIN' SERIES

A *Junior Library Guild* Selection

"Upbeat and heartfelt, Simon B. Rhymin' is a surefire hit!" —Lincoln Peirce, *New York Times* bestselling creator of Big Nate and Max & the Midknights

"Simon Barnes is my new favorite fifth-grade hero. He tackles tough issues with heartfelt sincerity while still making us smile with his rhythm and rhyme. Kids will love his story." —Liesl Shurtliff, *New York Times* bestselling author of *Rump*

★ "Reed writes his characters with compassionate and keen insight, effectively conveying the transformative power of art, storytelling, and community." —*Publishers Weekly*, starred review

"This uplifting, realistic story of a young Black boy lyricist is a strong addition to any library collection." —*School Library Journal*

"Dwayne Reed has done it again! This unforgettable protagonist will inspire young readers to utilize whatever skill and talent they possess." —Derrick Barnes, Newbery Honor author and two-time Kirkus Prize winner

"Change is possible and books like this one help remind us of exactly that. Within these pages you'll find courage, community, and some really, really great rhymes. I love Simon." —Brad Montague, *New York Times* bestselling author

"Readers encounter Simon's infectious personality, lively raps, warm, loving family, and collection of loyal friends....A timely tale that successfully blends the challenges of urban communities with hope and optimism." —*Kirkus Reviews*

SIMON B. RHYMIN'

TAKES A STAND

BY DWAYNE REED

WITH ELLIEN HOLI

ILLUSTRATED BY

ROBERT PAUL JR.

LITTLE, BROWN AND COMPANY
New York Boston

This book is a work of fiction. Names, characters, places, and incidents are the product of the author's imagination or are used fictitiously. Any resemblance to actual events, locales, or persons, living or dead, is coincidental.

Little, Brown and Company
Hachette Book Group
1290 Avenue of the Americas, New York, NY 10104
Visit us at LBYR.com

Originally published in hardcover and ebook by Little, Brown and Company in April 2022
First Trade Paperback Edition: March 2023

Little, Brown and Company is a division of Hachette Book Group, Inc. The Little, Brown name and logo are trademarks of Hachette Book Group, Inc.

The publisher is not responsible for websites (or their content) that are not owned by the publisher.

The Library of Congress cataloged the hardcover as follows:
Names: Reed, Dwayne, author. | Holi, Ellien, author. |
Paul, Robert, Jr., illustrator.
Title: Simon B. Rhymin' takes a stand / by Dwayne Reed with Ellien Holi ; illustrated by Robert Paul Jr.
Description: First edition. | New York : Little, Brown and Company, 2022. | Audience: Ages 8–12. | Summary: When Simon B. Rhymin' and his crew notice inequality in their school and neighborhood, they use rhymes to help bring their community together.
Identifiers: LCCN 2021016149 | ISBN 9780316539012 (hardcover) | ISBN 9780316539029 (ebook)
Subjects: CYAC: Social action—Fiction. | Rap (Music)—Fiction. | African Americans—Fiction.
Classification: LCC PZ7.1.R4278 Sm 2022 | DDC [Fic]—dc23
LC record available at https://lccn.loc.gov/2021016149

ISBNs: 978-0-316-53899-2 (pbk.),
978-0-316-53902-9 (ebook)

Printed in the United States of America

LSC-C

Printing 1, 2022

THIS ONE'S FOR YOU, KENDALL. IF SIMON TURNS OUT TO BE HALF THE RAPPER YOU WERE, HE'LL BE AIGHT. BETTER YET, HE'LL BE "PRECISE." LOVE YOU, BRO.

MONDAY

CHAPTER 1

OKAY, HEAR ME OUT: THERE'S A PER-fectly good reason for why I already look a mess before we've even gotten to school. And ain't none of it my fault. Cuz, like, I'm just a kid. *Ahem,* I mean, I'm still the Notorious D.O.G. and all, but that don't mean I can control the weather or nothin'. I also can't control Booker T. I mean, none of us can. It's a *whole* school.

First period starts at 8:01 a.m. so Moms always starts actin' like she's gonna bust down our doors around seven a.m. so we have enough time to wash up, get dressed, and eat something before we leave the house. Me, Markus, DeShawn, and Aaron all have to share a bathroom. Moms and Dad are only two people but they get a whole different bathroom that's much bigger inside their bedroom even though they don't even have to go to school every day. They don't even leave at the same time for work! I can't wait till I'm grown, like Moms calls me when she don't like my tone or thinks I got an attitude. When I'm grown, I'ma have fifteen bathrooms in my house and I won't have to share any of them!

Anyway, that's not the real problem. The real problem is getting dressed. Sure, Moms took me shopping the day before school started and all, but it ain't even about that. Let me break it down some more: When Moms took me shopping for school clothes, she bought me stuff for the fall and winter cuz it starts gettin' breezy pretty fast in the Chi. So she bought stuff like hoodies, joggers, jerseys, and a few T-shirts for what she calls the last breaths of summer.

Even though it's October now, and it should be getting chilly outside, we keep having extra-hot days like it's still August or something. And to make everything even worse, we can never tell what it's gonna feel like inside Booker T. Even Maria complains about not knowing how to dress because we never know what it's gonna feel like in class even though she says she loves the changing seasons—whatever that's supposed to mean. So when I finally catch up to Maria and Ms. Estelle, it feels extra shady that Maria can't stop laughing at how hard I tried to be extra prepared for most of the seasons to happen all in one day.

"OH EM GEEEEEE, Simon!" Maria and Ms. Estelle stop walking as I finally catch up to them halfway down Locust Street, out of breath and probably lookin' like I just played one-on-one with Aaron and got whupped. She makes a full circle around me, looking me up and down

with the weirdest smirk on her face. I know she's trying to think of something nice to say. "It's…um, different. I like it! You're way ahead of the game," she says, trying not to bust out laughing while pulling at my polo collar, then lifting up the hood of my hoodie like she might find something hiding under it. "But you're not hot?"

I look down, feeling all the clothes on top of each other, and know she's right. If I were a cartoon character, there'd be big flame waves coming off me.

HA—HA—HA, THEY THINK THE JOKE'S ON ME!
AND IT'S PROLLY CUZ I GOT A LOTTA CLOTHES
    ON ME.
LET ME SAY WHAT I MEAN: ROCKIN' DARK BLUE
    JEANS

WITH THE SHORTS UNDERNEATH, JUST IN CASE
    OF THE HEAT.

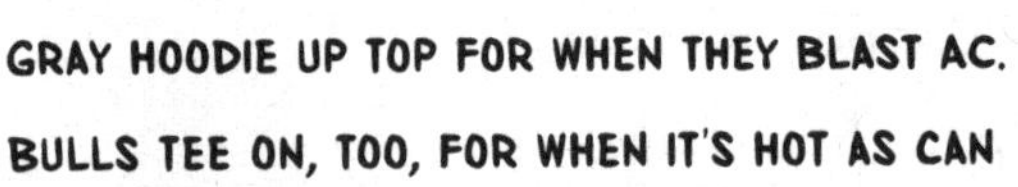

GRAY HOODIE UP TOP FOR WHEN THEY BLAST AC.
BULLS TEE ON, TOO, FOR WHEN IT'S HOT AS CAN
    BE.
NO HAT ON TODAY, BUT TOMORROW, WE'LL SEE

BECAUSE MY HEAD GETS COLD WHEN I'M IN
5--B.

IF IT'S BLAZIN' INSIDE, OR IF THEY GOT ON THE
AIR
THERE'S A JACKET IN MY BACKPACK, I'M ALWAYS
PREPARED.
SO LISTEN, I DON'T CARE IF I LOOK LIKE A SHOW
CUZ YA JUST NEVER KNOW HOW THE DAY'S GON'
GO.
WOOF!

We pass Mr. Ray's barbershop as we get closer to the school parking lot, and I check myself in the reflection of the window, immediately wishing I could run back home without being late. But Notorious D.O.G. ain't never late and ain't never scared.

"I was tryna be prepared," I mumble under my breath, starting to feel tired at the thought of dressing like this every day.

"Ay, Simon. Escuela started a whole month ago. You don't have all your supplies yet?!"

"That's not what he means, 'Buela," Maria says, turning behind us to answer Ms. Estelle for me.

I try to sneak a sniff under my left arm and breathe out extra hard, glad I ain't funky…yet.

"MISTA JAMES, I know what you gonna say but it's not my fault!" Even for Kenny, this scene is too much drama. He's busted into the class a whole five minutes late, and the way he screams his excuse, ain't no way Mr. James can teach without stopping to give him some attention. "My mama say I gotta stay hydrated and the line for the water fountain is *infinity-a-million* miles long, Mista James. She say she ain't got time to be leavin' work if I pass out cuz I don't have enough water in my body, okay?"

Mr. James wraps one arm across his chest and sits the opposite elbow on top of it, putting the bottom half of his face into his hand like he's trying not to laugh like the rest of the class already is. Don't nobody know why Lil Kenny could be late like this, even because of a long line. My guy looks like he rolled out of bed and walked straight to school. No teeth-brushing. No washing up. No changing into outside clothes. Straight to school, not even stopping to wipe the sleep out his eyes, like Moms calls it. His durag is still tied tight over his cornrows, and he's drowning in what looks like a grown-up's super-old white tee. If it wasn't for the few inches of his shorts peeking out at the bottom, I'd think he was under-dressed, even though it's hot outside. His shoes are the only things that make him look like he maybe tried a little bit. But even those are just some dusty old Nike slides that he wears with chunky white socks that are way too big for him. I can relate.

But still. Couldn't have taken more than five minutes to get ready. The dripping water around Lil Kenny's mouth, still making a trail down his chin. Lil Kenny always looks like he's wearing clothes that belong to somebody twice his size but maybe he was tryna be prepared, too.

"All right, Kenny. Your seat, now."

He wobbles to his seat, using his left hand to pull up his shorts that are obviously too big for him, dragging his Avatar backpack behind him with his right, plopping down with a loud yawn.

"As I was saying, prot—"

A loud thud, followed by a sharp kick, comes

from the ceiling and all of a sudden the class gets way too quiet.

"Awwww, MAAAN. Not this again!" Lil Kenny says like he was waiting for another reason to make us all look his way. But instead we all watch Mr. James walk over to the side of his desk, pick up the class fan, and take it to the window, which he opens and props the fan in without saying a word. He plugs it in and soon the noise that, minutes ago, was the AC is now the loud hum of a cheap fan that the school gave him a few weeks ago. This all only takes like a minute and we're all already wiping off beads of sweat that appeared the moment the AC shut off *again*. Yes, again. This is the drill almost every couple of days. Does Notorious D.O.G.'s layered look make more sense now?

I start pulling my hoodie up over my head, feeling proud of myself for being prepared, but I'm still annoyed. Why can't they fix it already?

A finger jabs my side just before my head escapes from under the bottom of my too-cold AC layer. Bobby pauses on his way to the front with his head turned around to make sure I know it was him. "Maybe you should just wear one outfit at a time, Simon. Your mom's gonna be mad if you get sweat all over your new school clothes before winter even gets here," he says with a smirk as he turns back around toward the door, where Mr. James is standing.

UGH! DIFFERENT DAY, BUT THE SAME OLD BOBBY!

HE NEEDS A NEW GAME, HE NEEDS A NEW HOBBY!

CUZ BULLYING ME IS GETTING OLD REAL FAST.

CAN'T HE GET SWITCHED TO A WHOLE 'NOTHER CLASS?

PLEASE!

"Back to your seat, Mr. Sanchez. Just cuz it's getting a little warm in here doesn't mean I can't see you walkin' all over my class."

"I be getting too cold in here," I whisper to Maria. At least that's the case when it works.

"But now it's hot again," she whispers back.

"That's why I got layers on, duh."

"*Fa-la-la-la-la-LAAAAAAAAAH,*" Kenny sings

into the fan blades, loud and slow. Kenny kneels on top of the table that sits under the window and takes in a deep breath for another long, robotic note made by his voice going through the fan. None of us even knows how or when he climbed up onto the table in front of the window but now none of us can stop laughing.

Mr. James turns out the lights. Kenny flips over, swings his short legs to fling hisself off the table, and runs to his seat, folding his fingers together like nothing even happened. Mr. James shakes his head as he walks over to turn on the SMART Board.

"Thas what I'm talkin' about! We finna go back to sleep, y'all!" Kenny blurts out, looking at the picture on the screen.

"That's enough, Kenny. Class, what do you see here?

"Like I sa—" Mr. James walks over to Kenny's desk and puts one hand on it. Kenny covers his own mouth with one hand and points to it with the other.

"It look like people sleeping on the street," somebody says.

"They took pillows out they bedroom and used it outside on the ground," somebody else says. Some more kids raise their hands, pointing at the screen, saying things like *They got blankets!* and *Maybe they don't have no house to sleep at like Mr. Sunny* and *They have signs and they eyes is closed!*

Maria reads what one of the signs on the ground says: "I SLEEP FOR BREONNA. Oo-oo-oo! I know that name, Mr. James!"

Mr. James walks away from Kenny's desk and to the front of the room, leaning his back on the chalkboard. For a minute I'm happy for Mr. James. Today he got on a black shirt with a red bow tie, and for once, the chalkboard doesn't have any chalk on it. That could have been all bad for the rappin' teacher's look.

"I know who that is, too!"

"Me too! That's the girl who used to be on the news!"

"Yeah, that's Breonna Taylor! She look just like my cousin Lisa, Mr. James," somebody else says.

"We all know that name by now, don't we? And the person who had that name looks like a lot of our family members, huh?" Mr. James's question makes me sit up in my seat a little.

"Yeah, we know that name, Mr. James. But why the people in the picture layin' in the street? How can cars get through if all those people are pretending to sleep in the street?" I ask.

"That's the point." Sometimes Mr. James sounds like he's speaking in riddles and I don't feel so smart, even though, one time, Aaron said that's why my head's so big. He said I know too much for my own good, whatever that means. "Do you think you could ignore all those people lying down in the street if you were in the car with your family trying to go somewhere? Would you still be able to go where you're going if they didn't move out of the way?"

"I guess not," I say, hearing myself sounding still confused.

"Would you want to know why they were lying there?"

"They need to get out the way or they gon' get ran over!" Lil Kenny strikes again.

"I would want to know," Maria says finally.

"I already do." That's when she turns around in her seat to look me in the eye. "Simon, don't you remember when we were watching the news with 'Buela that one summer and how the news people were talking about her? Don't you remember the people they were interviewing who kept saying it was taking too many days for her justice?"

"Yeah" is all I can say. I start to remember but everything feels blurry cuz I don't remember much happening after that.

"What did that sign say her name was?" Mr. James asks Maria, making her turn back around in her seat.

"Breonna."

"Her *full* name."

"Her name was Breonna Taylor," Maria tells him.

"That's right. Say her name, class."

BREONNA TAYLOR, I say with the class.

"Again."

BREONNA TAYLOR! we say loud enough for anyone who might be in the hall to hear.

"Those people were lying in the street so you all

can do what you're doing right now: remembering someone who suffered an injustice like her. They were lying in the street to bring attention to police brutality and demand an end to it. They were lying in the street to tell the world that what happened to Breonna Taylor isn't okay and that it needs to stop," said Mr. James, more serious than I've ever heard him sound.

"A protest!" Maria screams, almost jumping out of her seat. *That* is a protest? Marches and Martin Luther King Jr. and Rosa Parks speeches we did during Black History Month back in, like, the second grade start coming back to my brain but not people laying in the street. Not being... *quiet*. Every time we hear that word, people got they fists up, yelling.

"That's right, Maria. This is called a protest." Mr. James calls Maria up to the front to give her a stack of paper to hand out to the class. I sit staring at the picture of the people in the street while she walks around handing one to each of us. "This week we gon' explore different ways to protest or let the world or our community know something isn't okay with us and that we want it to stop. I've given each of you a different picture to study tonight for homework. I want a two-paragraph free-write about what you notice in your picture and some of your thoughts about what you see. What are the people in your picture fighting for? What are they doing that makes it a protest? Do you think it will work? What is something you would protest?"

A loud screech screams from the old intercom nailed to the wall above the class door like an angry bird. All our heads turn to look at it as Mr. James sits on the edge of his desk. It looks like it was built back when Sunny was a student at Booker T. and they never even tried to make it match how our school looks now. We hear Ms. Berry clear her throat into the mic before the announcements:

HAPPY MONDAY, BOOKER T. TODAY'S LUNCH IS CHICKEN NUGGETS, SEASONED FRENCH FRIES, YOUR CHOICE OF JUICE OR MILK, AND JELL-O FOR DESSERT. AS YOU MAY HAVE NOTICED, THE AC IS DOWN AGAIN. PLEASE BE SURE TO DRINK LOTS OF WATER TODAY. TEACHERS, PLEASE MAKE

TIME FOR TRIPS TO THE WATER FOUNTAIN. I WILL BE COMING AROUND TO SEE IF YOU NEED FANS AND WILL BRING THEM TO CLASSES IF ANY ARE AVAILABLE. MAKE IT A FANTASTIC DAY. HA-HA, FAN-TASTIC! GET IT?

Nobody laughs.

CHAPTER 2

"AIN'T NOTHING *FAN--TASTIC*, OR WHAT--ever, about that dusty fan they be making Mr. James use cuz the AC always broken," I tell C.J. while waiting for Mr. James to pass out recess equipment. We wait right by the doors that lead back outside.

"Yeah! Simon changed his whole look in class twice! It was like magic. Every period, a new look. Good planning ahead, friend!" Maria says this in the high pitch she uses when she's tryna get back on my good side.

"It's aight, Ri-Ri. Not everybody understands my genius!" I say, playing it cool. I turn toward

Mr. James, who's just walked up behind us with a big orange-netted bag full of kickballs, cones, and boxes of sidewalk chalk. Kids run toward us like magnets tryna get first dibs. Even though the younger kids are supposed to pick first, he has everybody make a line down the hall behind me. Maria and C.J. chill on the steps right outside the door, where I can still hear them.

"Mrs. Leary brought a fancy fan from her house. She still ain't figured out how to set it up in a place where it don't blow papers off her desk every day, though," C.J. says, tightening his second set of shoelaces. He leans back and puts his arms behind his head, pretending he's kicking his feet up in a recliner chair like the one at my granny's house, and adds: "And ain't none of us about to help her figure it out. We can't help that she old. Less homework for us! Haaaaa!"

Mr. James overhears C.J.'s shenanigans. "Aye, you gon' be old one day, too, lil man," he says, handing me a red kickball.

"Oh, nah, I'ma be like this forever! Y'all chumps can get wrinkly and weird if you want to!"

"But C.J., if you—ugh, never mind. Let's go before Bobby and his friends take over our favorite waaaaaall!" The way Maria takes off across the parking lot toward the end of her sentence without warning us is so funny that me and C.J. take even longer than we should have to meet her there cuz we're laughing so hard we're wheezing. From behind her, we see her use her left hand to hold her huge glasses—they're pink today—in place while she runs toward the giant brick wall that separates the playground with the wood chips from the sidewalk on Locust. The other hand, with its fingers wrapped tight around the handle of her water bottle, bounces around at her side like a fish that just got caught but is still alive on the hook. I'd know. Dad took me and my brothers down to the lake once. Notorious D.O.G. thought he was gon' fall in so he just stayed behind Dad. Don't tell nobody. Anyway, Maria. Like a wiggly fish. Running. Hilarious.

I catch a second wind and take off behind her.

"What the—" is all I hear from C.J. before he's too far behind us. I zig and I zag through parked cars, coaching my confused homie behind me, yelling "Let's go!" and "I know you not about to let me beat you!" back at C.J. like I'd ever let him catch up to me or beat me to the wall. I slap hands with Maria while C.J., completely out of breath, finally makes it over. He could probably be in one of the soap operas Moms be watchin' the way he slams into the wall, drops to his knees, and stretches out on the ground. Maria reaches out to poke his side.

"Aye! Back up!" he screams. We all bust out laughing while C.J. sits up and starts getting himself together.

"Say it," Maria orders.

"Dang, can a brother at least catch his breath first?"

"OH EM *GEEEEE*, you're taking forever, though! C'mon! You know the rules."

Out of the three of us, C.J. hates the rules the most. Last one to the wall must sing our praises. Too bad it's him about 75 percent of the time. He never suspects that we're about to trick him. He's too...nice. "Ugh, fine." Robotically, and like the sentences are the silliest words he's ever tasted, he squeezes our compliments out through his teeth with a goofy smirk. *"Maria, oh queen of everything. You are the best debater in the world. Oh, Notorious D.O.G., the best rapper alive. No one is as cold as you."*

Me and Maria snort, trying hard to keep our faces straight, but the minute he gets the last word out we fall on each other laughing and then bowing repeatedly at our compliments. Even though it's a competition and nobody likes to lose, it gives the Notorious D.O.G. a little extra confidence, low-key. Sometimes I let C.J. win so he can see how good it feels, too. Sometimes he really beats me on the days my AC layers get to be too much and I'm too tired to try.

He bends over to brush small rocks off his legs and his elbows, then finally wipes the sweat off his forehead with the back of his arm. "But yo. I feel kinda like Mrs. Leary, no cap. This morning she had to sit down in the middle of class after the AC broke again. We was hot but not *that* hot," he says with his eyes getting all big. Maria drops the kickball and slaps it up toward the top of the wall. "Couldn't even see her head no more when I raised my hand to go to the water fountain. Had to look past Jerrell Wright's Afro to see if she was gon' let me go. You know how he be pickin' it out all day."

Jerrell Wright is one of those kids who came back to school looking extra different. Back in the fourth grade he kept getting his brush taken away cuz he was always workin' on his 360-degree waves around the clock—even in school. This year he got way more hair and, instead of a brush, it's a super-long pick that he keeps stuck in his hair when he's not using it. C.J. slaps the ball back up against the wall when it drops in front of him.

"Lil Kenny made a whole scene about the water fountain, too," I say, realizing Kenny might not have been acting as dramatic as I thought.

"Longest line ever! And when it was finally my turn, I didn't even wanna drink out of it. Looked kinda...gross." This is one of the first times I hear C.J. making a big deal about something being clean. That's usually Maria's thing. "You think they ever clean it?"

"Probably not. That's why 'Buela got me a water

bottle. I'm never even getting close to that thing. *So* nasty. Half the times kids have to put their whole face down to get enough water. It don't look like it even really works," she says, scrunching up her face, almost missing the ball as it comes down in front of her.

"My cousin Phil never has these problems at his school on the North Side. They even got snack machines in their *real* cafeteria," C.J. says, shaking his head. "You could buy Reese's, Butterfingers, Flamin' Hots…" For a second he drifts off into space while saying the names of all his favorite snacks.

I WISH WE HAD FANCIER THINGS AT THIS
SCHOOL.
ANOTHER WATER FOUNTAIN, AC WOULD BE COOL!
EXTRA SUPPLIES AND HEALTHIER SNACKS,

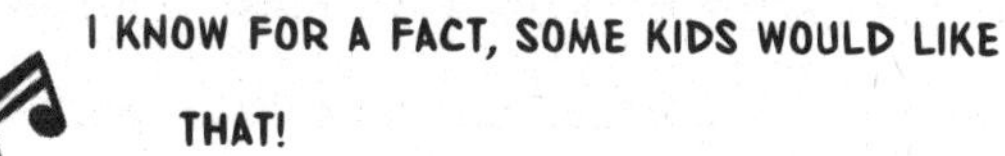

I KNOW FOR A FACT, SOME KIDS WOULD LIKE
THAT!

BUT ME AND C.J., BRO, WE WANT THE JUNK
FOOD

INSTEAD OF THAT NASTY AND OLD LUNCH FOOD.
WE WANT ALL THE SWEETS AND TASTIER TREATS.
I WISH BOOKER T. GAVE US THAT TO EAT!
LIKE SNICKERS AND TWIX AND CHICK-O-STICKS
AND SKITTLES WITH ALL OF THE RAINBOW MIXED
AND FROOTIES AND CHEWS AND BAGS OF CHIPS,
DORITOS WITH CHILI AND CHEESE TO DIP,
AND TAKIS TO LICK, AND FANTA TO SIP,
AND ALL OF THE SNACKS, AND ALL OF THE DRIP,
AND MUSIC ON BLAST IN THE HALL AS WE PASS
AND A VENDING MACHINE IN EVERY CLASS
AND A TV SCREEN AND A TRAMPOLINE
AND A PLACE FOR THE KIDS WHO ARE ALWAYS MEAN!
YEAHHHH, I WISH WE HAD FANCIER THINGS.
IT WOULD BE NICE TO HAVE FANCIER THINGS!

"C.J.!"

"Wha—oh! Yeah, anyway. I know they don't make kids do performances, gym class, *and* lunch all in the same little auditorium at fancier schools." A basketball flies over Maria's head and C.J. catches it, slapping the kickball before it can hit the ground, on accident.

"AH! AH! AH! You out!" I try to tell him.

"Nah! That don't count. I was saving Maria's life!" Maria rolls her eyes, picking up the kickball and holding it between her hip and her hand.

"My *life*? You ain't save nobody, C.J. Rules is rules. Simon's right. You can be my cheerleader, though. Mira!" Maria gets into ready position to keep playing like she's about to football or something. She looks a little silly but nobody's cockier than her.

"Listen to your very miniature friend, C.J. That big head might actually have something in it," Bobby interrupts, snatching the basketball out of C.J.'s hand. Bobby looks me up and down for a second, then pushes past C.J. a little too rough, but without saying anything else. Does Bobby Sanchez *ever* wake up on the right side of the bed? Sheesh.

WHAT IF BOBBY WOKE UP ON THE RIGHT SIDE OF
THE BED?
MAYBE THEN HE WOULDN'T EVER TALK ABOUT MY
HEAD!
WHAT IF ALL HIS SHEETS WERE CLEAN WITH
PILLOWS SOFT AS BREAD?

WOULD THAT HELP HIM BE A LOT NICER WITH
THE STUFF HE SAID?

I BET YOU IF HE GOT REST HE WOULDN'T BE SO
CRANKY.
HE'D PROLLY BE MORE HAPPY AND HE PROLLY
WOULDN'T HATE ME.
AND MAYBE, JUST MAYBE, WE WOULD ALL BE
COOL
IF HE WOKE UP ON THE RIGHT SIDE OF THE BED
BEFORE SCHOOL.

"I think it's like this at the high school, too," I say, picking up from where C.J. left off. "They don't got a lot of space, either, but at least they let them use the basketball court up the street and the rec center in Garfield Park instead of only letting them bounce basketballs around at recess like Bobby does." Even those are a little rough. The Chicago Bulls would *never* play ball on a court with hoops that got chains instead of nets. I bet they'd never even look at a backboard with paint so chipped we can barely see the square above the hoop. But really, they probably had to before anybody discovered them, right? "One time Sunny told me that court used to be part of Booker T.'s yard when it was safe to walk through the park." The kickball flies toward my head and I punch it into the air.

"This is wall ball, not a boxing match, Simon! I win," Maria announces as soon as my fist comes back down. Ugh. For a second, I forgot what we were doing.

"I—I was tryna show y'all how far I could get the ball off the ground." They both stand there staring at me and then look at each other. I try something else. "I—I was showing y'all what I'ma do to Bobby next time he try to test the Notorious D.O.G.," I say, knowing the end of what I say sounds more like a guess than the truth.

This time Maria crosses her arms and smirks. C.J. shakes his head, walks to grab the ball, and says what Maria's probably thinking. "Simon ain't 'bout to fight nobody."

"Uggghh. Whatever! That means this round's over and we still got some time for me to whup both of y'all. Let's go," I say, cracking my knuckles. I throw in random stretches I've seen Aaron do after playing ball so they know I mean business. What stretches? I mean, does it even matter? Maria turns to take a sip from her water bottle and I see my chance. The kickball flies high up and taps the wall before coming down in front of her as she turns back to face me and C.J. She panics, thinking it's gonna drop on her head, and smacks it before it can hit the ground, as planned. Me and C.J. scream and run circles around her, asking her "How does it feel to lose?" and "YOU MAD OR NAH?" and "What will you do with your life now that wall ball is no longer your thing?"

"Y'all just mad cuz I usually win, " Maria says, barely reacting to our gloating. She takes another big gulp out of her water bottle, shooing us off like annoying little flies that she can't be bothered with. "My cousin Lorena told me, at her school, they all got their own laptops to take home to do homework."

"For real?!" me and C.J. blurt out at the same time.

"Yah, but like, I don't care that much cuz you don't need fancy computers to debate," Maria continues, looking like she's not even thinkin' about us or anybody else today. It even looks like she's smiling a little. The bell rings for us to get back inside.

Just before the second bell rings for the next period to start, Maria turns around in her seat to make sure I remember: "Don't forget, Simon. 'Buela's not coming until four thirty to pick me up from Debate Club. You gotta walk home with Aaron."

No wonder Maria couldn't be bothered this morning. She's been waiting all summer for her first Debate Club meeting. Not even another broken AC could ruin it.

TUESDAY

CHAPTER 3

I'VE NEVER SEEN WARNINGS ON THE Fruity-O's box before but I think there should be one for fifth graders who can't handle surprises. Yeah, it might be on there for babies, but the Notorious D.O.G. skipped that cuz it don't apply to me. It needs to be one specifically for times like this morning when somebody bangs on your front door without warning and you inhale so hard everything in your mouth goes in reverse. Chunks of cereal get stuck in the back of my throat, and milk somehow jumps from my throat up into my nose, spraying out as I cough for air. And it burns. Who knew there was a tunnel in there connecting your mouth and nose? Probably Maria. But I don't think she cares about any of that the way she's beating on the front door this morning.

Dad peeks through the peephole, turns around without opening it, and walks back to the sink, where he was doing dishes before he discovered Maria on the other side. I wipe the snotty milk off my upper lip with the back of my hand as he tells me, "It's for you, Si. And tell your little friend there's no need to be bustin' down the door so early in the morning." I hop off my kitchen stool, grab my cereal bowl that's only got sugary milk in it now, and gulp it down before putting the bowl on the side of the sink that's full of dirty breakfast dishes.

"Thanks, Dad."

"Yeah, yeah. This is gon' be your job tonight, son," he reminds me, before mushing the side of my face with a soapy hand. Both Moms and Dad always make sure that me and my brothers never forget that neither of them is our maid, but sometimes Dad likes to do stuff around the kitchen while he listens to music or shows with his headphones on so he can be in his own world. I feel like that sometimes when clever lyrics pop into my head that I think would make a crowd go crazy if I could just get myself to perform the stuff in real life. I wipe the wet side of my face with the back of my other hand while I run to finally open the door for Maria.

I LOVE MY WALKS WITH MARIA IN THE MORNIN'.
I CAN'T WAIT FOR THEM, THEY'RE NEVER, EVER
BORIN'.
I GET TO BE ME ON THE WAY TO BOOKER T.
AS I ROLL WITH RI--RI, AND OF COURSE, MS. E,
WALKING WITH MY HOMIE REALLY GETS ME ON
MY WAY.

CUZ EVEN IF IT'S CLOUDY, WITH HER, IT'S NEVER
GRAY.
WE JOKE AROUND A LOT AND YOU KNOW WE
GOTTA PLAY.
YEAH, IT'S A DOPE START TO AN ORDINARY DAY.

"We don't have time for you to be changing one million times today, okay, Simon? Ugh, you still don't even have your shoes on yet?! Gosh, I swear you must be *trying* to make us late," Maria says through her teeth. If I wasn't looking at my friend with my own eyes, I'd swear that it was Moms fussing at me and my brothers right now. Maria's got her left hand on her hip and her right hand gripped tight around the strap of her backpack. While shaking her head she continues, "Ay-ay-ay, Simon! Don't just stand there! ¡Vámonos!"

Okay, who is this person? Her pink frames slide down her nose as she barks the last word at me and when she doesn't push them back up, I know we got problems. Yesterday they were pink. Today was supposed to be a different color. And letting herself look old and mean like this? My best friend would never. Right now she sounds like a stranger. Something's wrong.

The last time Maria wore the same color glasses two days in a row was in the second grade. I haven't seen this Maria since the day our second-grade teacher, Ms. Hines, put the wrong times table quiz on Maria's desk by accident. It was only a few seconds before the bell was gonna ring and Ms. Hines put down a quiz marked with a big red *65%* on the top. The bell rang and Maria's face turned the color of the mark. The rest of the day she complained me and C.J. were chewing with our mouths open at lunch, told us we took too long to meet her outside for recess, and shooshed us whenever we laughed at something in class, even when it was supposed to be funny. The next morning when her and Ms. Estelle got to my door, she was wearing the same pair of baby-blue frames she was wearing the day before and she looked like she hadn't slept for weeks! She probably would have worn them a third day in a row if Ms. Hines didn't grab her first thing that morning to apologize for mixing the quiz scores up. The *65%* actually belonged to Marissa, a girl who slept through class most days.

I grab my backpack on the way out the door and lock it as fast as I can. No time to think through the perfect amount of layers to be ready for whatever seasons we might go through inside Booker T. today.

When I get to the sidewalk downstairs, one annoyed Maria is standing with her arms crossed beside Ms. Estelle, and I'm ready to find out what could be so bad that it put my best friend in such a weird mood. The second she sees me, she doesn't bother waiting for me before crossing the street. Ms. Estelle looks up at me and shrugs. "Hold up, Maria! Come on, you know I'm not as fast as you," I say, hoping she laughs, thinking about the way she dusted me and C.J. at recess yesterday.

She doesn't. She don't even try to slow down, either. I have to jog a little to finally catch up to her halfway up the block. I jump in front of her, turning around to face her with my hands out like I'm guarding somebody on the basketball court. Think: arms out like I'm a human stop sign, my knees bent like I'm about to sit on the toilet, but sticking out the way I once saw Aaron doing when he was doin' squats tryna get buff this summer. Don't worry, nobody else was around to see me. "Maria!"

"What is it, Simon? We're gonna be late."

"Nuh-uh. We're early. I know cuz I normally woulda had time to throw on *at least* two more AC layers." It's true. "You mad at me?"

"I don't know what you're talking about,"

she says, kinda like I'm a stranger, trying to step around me.

"Then why didn't you wait for me?"

"Oh please. Nobody has time to wait on you again, Simon." She crosses her hands over her chest, starts tapping her foot, and looks to the side. Looking past her glasses, I see gray bags under her eyes and water welling up behind them. She's pretending. "We just can't be late. If kids keep being late, somebody might think we don't need our school and take that away, too."

"What?"

"Nothing."

"It's not—"

"I don't know why they even made a Debate Club if they won't even let us compete! What's the point?!" The water spills all the way out of her eyelids now. I don't move. "It's so stupid." I still know I shouldn't make any quick moves. More is com—

"AND ANOTHER THING: How can we even practice with all those kids everywhere, playing dodgeball and throwing their stuff on our table like we weren't even sitting there?! Why would they take Mr. James's room for a meeting when we have practice so we had to have debate practice in the auditorium just so he could tell us our school doesn't have enough money for us to be a real team like other schools?!"

"Wait, what?" I can't think of anything better to say. I'm still a little confused, but it *does* sound bad.

"Did you hear me, Simon? No debate *team.* Only Debate Club."

I don't like seeing Maria cry, because she's usually so happy. She's usually the one who cheers *me* up. I don't like hearing my best friend tell me that her debate team has been downgraded to a debate club. That all the trips to other schools around the city, and state in the spring, are canceled.

"It's fine, because I'm gonna fix it!"

"Fix it how, Ri-Ri?"

But she was already walking into the school.

CHAPTER 4

"MM, YES. THANK YOU VERY MUCH," LIL Kenny says, leaning over C.J.'s shoulder and the edge of our table. He reaches out toward the smallest square on C.J.'s lunch tray with his left hand and uses his right hand to reach toward mine.

"Bruh. What do you think you're doin'?" C.J. asks for both of us.

"Tater Tots are in the vegetable group. Y'all give me the veggies y'all ain't tryna eat every day." Me and C.J. look at each other. "Yeah, I'm onto y'all. I just thought I'd come over and get mines now. Y'all always be givin' me cold stuff. We gotta work on that." When we both look at him like we've never even seen him before, he adds: "Aye, man, don't try to switch up on me now." His hands still float over our lunches like he's a little bit afraid of grabbing things too fast.

TATER TOTS ARE VEGETABLES?
THIS IS UNACCEPTABLE!
HOW CAN SOMETHING SO HEALTHY
BE SO DELECTABLE?
HOW CAN SOMETHING SO DELICIOUS
ALSO BE NUTRITIOUS?
SOME THINGS ARE SO SUSPICIOUS.
MAN, SOME THINGS ARE SO SUSPICIOUS.

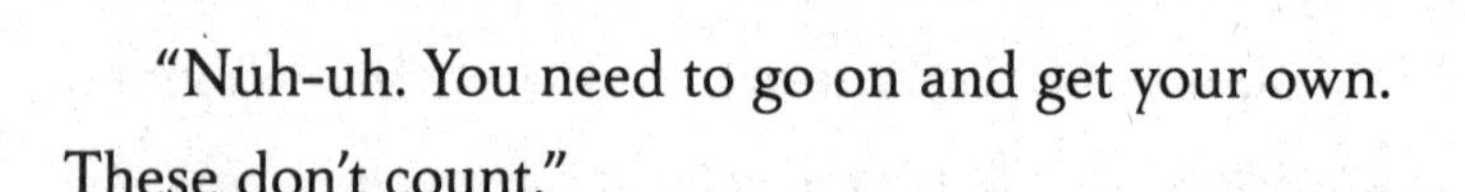

"Nuh-uh. You need to go on and get your own. These don't count."

"But it ain't no other veggies on the menu today!"

"We know, Kenny. But we want these. Maybe next time." C.J.'s already started opening all the little sauce packets so he can mix them together for the ultimate dipping sauce. Kenny looks over at me to see if I want to keep my Tater Tots, too.

"Maybe next time, Kenny."

Kenny shakes his head and starts backing away just as Maria finally gets to our table. "Y'all wrong for this. I'ma remember this next time you need my help with homework!"

"Boy, ain't nobody checkin' for you," Maria says loudly without even looking at Kenny, sounding a lot meaner than usual. He doesn't say anything, and she snaps again: "You don't even do your homework for real!"

"Yeah, well…well…that's cuz I'm doin' more important things!" he yells over the cafeteria noise, backing farther away from our table. By the end of lunch period, somebody's gonna give Lil Kenny their Tots. He might not do his homework but he's clever and isn't afraid to talk to anybody. Maria unpacks her SHE-ro lunch box in silence, slamming it onto the table like it's the head of whoever decided to ruin the debate team. No need to catch C.J. up on this, either. Normally when Maria's in a bad mood she'd rather be by herself, but there's only three seats left open at our table and, even while mad, she knows not to sit on the wobbly seat that's farthest away from us. She plops down next to C.J., opens a bowl of rice, and starts moving beans around. We stare at Michelle Obama's face on Maria's lunch box lid, which feels like a big ol' wall today, for almost five minutes. When she still doesn't say anything, C.J. takes the fruit cocktail off my tray and slides both his and mine over to her.

"Don't worry, you ain't the only one."

"Did I say I was the only one?! Ugh, C.J., you just don't—"

"I don't what?"

"You don't get it," both me and Maria say. The first time all day that it feels like we're okay. She fumbles with some papers in her hand while C.J. tries to defend himself.

"Why y'all always think I don't know stuff? I *know* tons of stuff is getting shut down. Deijah came home cryin' with snot all over her face after school cuz she can't do Karate Club no more. Not really. She told my mama that they makin' kids from Karate Club join Gymnastics Club instead."

"Yeah, well, it looks like, at Booker T., all

Gymnastics Club is, is letting *all* the kids flip, run, and throw dodgeballs at each other on the mats we use for gym class. I didn't even see any teachers except for Mr. James," Maria says, now moving her rice and beans around in the bowl. She finally takes a little bite. Both me and C.J.'s pizza is gone, and C.J.'s mystery sauce is a big circle on his tray waiting for him to dunk into. He dunks a handful of Tots and stuffs them all into his mouth at the same time.

"Well, it's no more Karate Club, Art Club, or Theater Club. Mrs. Leary says we could stay after school to paint in the art room while she does other stuff but ain't nobody tryna hang out with Mrs. Leary," he says through a stuffed mouth. I try not to look right at him while he's chewing and talking at the same time. It doesn't work unless I look away. "Anyway... it's big changes for everybody, Maria!" He takes a huge gulp of his chocolate milk to wash down the Tots and wipes off the drizzle coming down the side of his face with the back of his hand.

Jerrell stops by with a purple basketball on his hip. He must have brought that from home. They slap right hands into a shake, and Jerrell immediately uses the same hand to pick out the front of his Afro like the handshake messed it up.

"So, wassup? You tryin' out for the team or what?" he asks C.J., like they talked about it before.

"I don't know, man. I don't know."

"Well, you know I'ma be there," Jerrell reminds him, pushing his basketball up into the air, pretending to shoot it into an imaginary hoop. C.J. goes back to inhaling the rest of his lunch when Jerrell walks away. He swallows, shaking his head and chuckling to himself, and starts back up again.

"Like I was say—"

"Yeah, *C.J.*, are you going out for the basketball team *or naaaah*?" Maria asks, interrupting him and dragging out the "nah" part as much as she can. "Looks like not *everything* is getting shut down." C.J. isn't getting it and Maria is *over* it.

I have one million questions that come into my head all at the same time. Won't they have to share the court next to the barbershop? Nah, don't nobody practice outside on the West Side. "What y'all gonna do? Practice at Garfield Rec? Everybody be over there. Where the games gon' be?" And part of me is hype that one of my best friends is gon' be on a real basketball team!

"Probably in the auditorium, I don't know" is all C.J. says, still focused on finishing all his Tater Tots before recess.

Maria throws her hands up. "IN THE SAME AUDITORIUM WHERE DEBATE CLUB MEETS?! THE SAME ONE WHERE THEY HAVE GYMNASTICS?! *OH EMM GEEEEEEE!*" She's standing up now, with her eyes all big and her hands still up in the air with her fingers spread wide. If she was a cartoon character, there would be all kinds of steam coming out both of her ears and she'd probably be the color of a tomato. She actually already is.

"I mean, at least one of us gets to try out for a real team that gets to play against other teams," I say without thinking. Maria plops back down and I feel her sort of shrink in her seat. She doesn't say anything to that, and I try to fix it. "If they don't have money for *every*body, where's all the money going? Didn't they have all these clubs last year?"

"Maybe they gon' fix the water fountains once and for all," C.J. says.

"Probably not. The water fountain's been like that since the beginning of time," Maria finally says, taking her first real bite since lunch started. Neither me or C.J. knows what to say, so we watch her take a long, dramatic sip from her water bottle. I notice that she's still got the stack of papers she was shuffling a second ago now sitting next to her food. With one elbow on top of it, it almost feels like it's top secret or something. I start to ask her what it is but we all hear a basketball hitting the ground get closer to our table and for a second I forget it's still the middle of lunchtime.

All of a sudden Bobby and Victor G. are passing a basketball—that they obviously stole from the recess bag—back and forth above our heads and across the table. Feeling the wind of the basketball being passed so close to our heads makes me a little scared to move or stand up. I mean, *ahem,* the Notorious D.O.G. don't feel like leaving for recess just yet. Mr. James sees what's happening before I have to lay the smackdown. Somehow his hand reaches over our table mid-pass and the ball is in his hands.

"Y'all know we don't play ball in the cafeteria during lunch, right, fellas? Take a walk.... I'll hold on to this. I'm sure we'll need it for *recess.*" Mr. James always sounds way too nice but like he don't play no games at the same time. He's not really asking a question but Bobby says something back anyway.

"Cafeteria? You mean the gym? Or is this the auditorium today?" Bobby spits back. Mr. James palms the ball in one hand and starts walking back to the doorway that he was watching everybody from. Bobby and Victor walk off while more questions start filling my head. If Booker T. needs to save money for whatever so bad, how come they haven't canceled basketball around here? I mean, it's not a lot of space for that, either, but I haven't seen any ballplayers walking around as mad as Maria. Even if they probably have to share the court, at least they get uniforms and still get to play.

Maria's gone. Or at least she's not sitting across from me anymore. I slide my last Tater Tot across the little puddle of ketchup on my tray and throw it in my mouth. Just as I get ready to dump my tray, I spot Maria across the cafeteria talking to a bunch of kids I don't think I've ever seen, at a table we've never sat at! What's going on here?

For a second I just plop back down in my seat and watch my best friend go from one table to another and then to another before I stop tryna play it cool. *What is she doiiing?* "Yo, Ri-Ri! We not in class! What you tryna do, homework? We gon' miss first dibs on the ball wall. And you know we can't have none of that! I gotta beat y'all today!" Like I said, I stopped tryna play it cool when my friend started going to strange lunch tables. I gotta figure out what's up!

She looks back at me, with a face even more tomato-ey than before, shrugs, and storms back over with two hands full of those papers she had earlier. But now they look sort of like...she pulled them out of the garbage after somebody balled them up and threw them out. Somehow Mr. James magically appears back next to our table. With Bobby.

"Forget it!" she says when she finally makes it back to us.

"Wait, wait, wait...Maria, hold on. Bobby got somethin' he needs to say."

"Mr. James, you told us to pick up any papers left behind and put 'em in the trash!" Bobby says to Mr. James instead of talking to Maria. Bruh, I thought we lost these guys already.

"Bobby, do I look like I was born yesterday?" Mr. James asks, looking at Bobby like he knows *everything*. I mean, he do be knowin' a lot of times.

Bobby can't help himself. "I mean...you do be comin' in here with sneakers on like you—"

"Bobby" is all Mr. James says, stopping Bobby before he's mean to a teacher.

"All riiiight. Uh, my bad. My bad for throwing your stuff in the garbage. It *looked* like—"

Mr. James doesn't let Bobby finish. He looks

over by the door where he'd been standing, watching everybody during lunch, and Ms. Berry nods back at him, waving Bobby over to her. Bobby don't even try to tell everybody he didn't do anything. He just walks away with his fists all crumpled up. Before I can ask Maria what's going on, Mr. James is already kneeled down.

"Hey, hey, hey...deep breaths. Let me see those," he says, opening his hands so Maria can put the mystery papers in them. "Wow! Check you out. I knew I had some rising leaders in my class and you provin' it every day." He continues smiling at Maria while the bright red slowly starts turning light pink. "But look. You got *great friends* and what you tryna do takes community." All right, now I *need* to know what's goin' on!

"What are those, Maria?" I ask.

"Nothing," she says, looking like she don't wanna answer nobody. "I mean...not nothing... it's a petition. I was trying to get those kids over there to sign it," she says, pointing behind her without looking. Where did I hear that word before? *Petition*...

"It's *definitely* not nothing. Remember, this is one of the ways you can get things done when you want it to be known that a lot of people agree with you," Mr. James says, sort of like I should have known all this stuff. He turns so he's facing all three of us and stands back up so C.J., who's been behind us trying to straighten some of the crinkled-up papers that dropped to the floor when Maria stormed back across the cafeteria, can hear him, too. "But Maria's gonna need y'all's help. I know y'all are tight. Sis can't do it all by herself."

I pull one of the sheets of paper from under C.J.'s hands and see Maria's handwriting at the top of each one and a bunch of lines drawn under it.

"We gotta fight this, guys. They can't take away all our clubs. It's not fair," she tells us all. Somehow Lil Kenny reappears with his arms crossed like he's ready to watch whatever's about to go down even though there's nothin' else to see. C.J. stands up from his seat to take his tray to the garbage and Mr. James tells us both to leave our stuff there.

"Bobby and Victor will be hanging out with me in here for a little bit while y'all enjoy your recess."

He winks at us and walks off. Before I can open my mouth, Maria's halfway across the cafeteria following after Mr. James. Guess they gotta talk about *leader* stuff. I know Mr. James heard her say *fight* but he didn't seem like he had a problem with it. Notorious D.O.G.'s never been in a real fight before, but maybe his first will be in the fifth grade.

I AIN'T NEVER EVER FOUGHT A PERSON IN MY
LIFE.

I PLAYED A BOXING GAME,
UP--DOWN--LEFT--RIGHT.

I WRESTLED WITH MY BROTHERS AND WE HAD A
PILLOW FIGHT.
BUT I'VE NEVER USED MY HANDS FOR ANYTHING
EXCEPT TO WRITE.

ME? FIGHTING? THAT'S GOT ME KINDA CURIOUS!
I'M WAY TOO SMALL--WHO WOULD EVER TAKE ME
SERIOUS?
I DON'T EVEN SPEAK WHENEVER BOBBY GETS TO
CAPPIN',
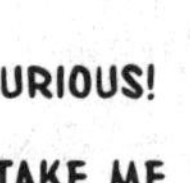
SO IMAGINE WHAT WOULD HAPPEN IF SOME
FINGERS GET TO SMACKIN'?

IF KNUCKLES GET TO CRACKIN', IF HANDS GET TO
SLAPPIN',
I'D PROLLY JUST HIDE INSTEAD OF JOININ' IN
THE ACTION.
BUT MARIA'S TALKING 'BOUT SOME "GUYS, WE
GOTTA FIGHT!"
DOES SHE EVEN UNDERSTAND THAT I AM NOT
THE FIGHTING TYPE?!

I AM NOT THE ONE FOR VIOLENCE, I WON'T EVER
TAKE A SWIPE.
I WOULD RATHER TAKE A STEP BACK INSTEAD OF
GETTIN' HYPE.
MARIA, I SUPPORT YOU, AND I WANT TO DO
WHAT'S RIGHT,
BUT JUST CUZ I'M THE D.O.G., THAT DOESN'T
MEAN I BITE!
WOOF WOOF!

CHAPTER 5

I'VE BEEN STARING AT THIS PICTURE OF Colin Kaepernick that Mr. James gave me for like twenty whole minutes and all I can think about is how the smell of Dad's famous catfish is about to fill up our whole apartment. The way it hits the oil and sizzles and turns brown and how flaky it is when it's fried just right. I stare at it a little longer and I start smelling crinkly fries. All I need is some bread to—

"Simon, baby, hellooooooo." Moms is leaned over the other side of the kitchen counter and she's looking at me like she's seriously worried. "For a minute there I thought I was gon' have to pour some ice water on! You all right, son?"

I shake my head and snap out of whatever world I was in before Moms brought me back to reality: me and her at the kitchen counter with my protest assignment, Dad off to the side dipping pieces of fish in a bowl with headphones on, off in his own world. No bread to go with it in sight.

"Why don't you take a brain break? You look like you're working a little too hard over there."

Parents are so confusing. Most of the time they're going off about cleaning up around the house or reminding us homework comes before TV or any type of fun at all. Now Moms is telling me my brain should take a break like Mr. James does when nobody in class knows the answers to one of his deep questions. And I'm not even close to being done yet. I can't keep up! At least it buys me some time before I have to think about what to say about this picture he gave me for homework. So far all I got is "He real mad at somebody and it look like football is the furthest thing from his mind."

If by "too hard" Moms means "not at all," she's

right. I put the picture down and see she's already turned back around to dump the purple cabbage she made DeShawn chop for her into a huge pot of boiling water. She picks up an even bigger pot and pours chopped potatoes over a thing with holes in it and a big cloud of steam covers her head and floats up to the ceiling. I start to forget Dad is in here with us, till he laughs out loud to himself about something neither me or Moms can hear.

"These jokers is some fools!" The way he wheezes after he lets out the first part of his laugh would make you think he's sick or something, but it's never that. He just laughs harder than everybody else, which is kinda cool when I think about how serious everybody's dads are. Dad bends over, slaps his knee, then stands up straight again, waving his pointer finger in the air. Ever since Moms bought him these fancy headphones to listen to his podcasts on, he almost always forgets anybody's around. *That's why I give him something to do BEFORE he puts them thangs on,* she always says to me while they're cooking.

Moms dumps the potatoes into another bowl and puts the steamy bowl in front of me, handing me a masher. "I heard mashing things is good stress relief. Get busy."

I use all the muscles in my arms with my fingers wrapped around the handle. I'm kneeling on the stool I was sitting on, leaned over the counter while she watches me turn the chopped potatoes into a thick, creamy, whitish fluff. The same steam that covered Moms' head covers my face so much it looks like I'm sweating.

"That's perfect," she says, shooing me away from the bowl when she's ready for me to stop. She probably didn't want my face juice dropping into the bowl. Good call, Moms. When she hands me a paper towel to dry off my face, it reminds me of Maria's face this morning.

"I think Maria is mad at me. I mean *us.* I mean…," I start to tell her, feeling confused all of a sudden about who Maria is mad at.

"You *think* or you know?" Moms pushes, adding half a stick of butter to the bowl and lifting one of her eyebrows.

"I don't know. She was crying this morning because she said her debate team won't get to compete and she said I wasn't listening. She was even mean to Lil Kenny at lunch and he didn't even do nothin' to her." It's true. It's hard to tell who she's mad at because none of us knows who did this to our school. "She just looked so sad, and Maria's never sad."

"Well, did she tell you why that happened to her team?"

"She said the school doesn't have the money."

"Uh-huh."

"And...and then C.J. said the school is taking a lot of money away from people's clubs. I feel bad."

"Uh-huh." I wish Moms would say something else besides *Uh-huh*.

"But not the basketball team, though! They're not getting cut. And Maria was just so upset. It's not fair, Mom. I don't know how to help her."

"Simon, you know where that cabbage and

these potatoes came from?" she asks. *This ain't the time for one of your speeches about how you and Dad work hard to put food on the table for us, Moms. Focus.*

"Um...from the store?"

"Before that."

"Um...the ground?"

"Bingo. A lot of the vegetables we cookin' right now and many in the fridge came from the Creighton Community Garden," she says with a proud smile, pausing like she wants me to say something. I still don't know what's going on.

"What garden? I never saw any...Wait, what does this have to do with—"

"Behind the shelter. On the next block over on Claude Street is the garden me and your auntie Julia *fought* to have in this community. There was a time when me and your daddy had to go across town to get fresh vegetables cuz they weren't delivering none to *our* grocery store. And they had the nerve to try to build another one of them liquor stores over there. We weren't havin' it."

Just like I don't know who Maria is mad at, I

don't know who the *they* is that Moms is talking about. "Mama. You was in a fight with the grocery store people?!"

She doesn't even pretend to not laugh at me. "No, baby. We weren't *in* a fight. We *fought* for our right to have fresh food."

THAT CAN'T BE POSSIBLE, NO, THAT CAN'T BE RIGHT!
MOMS WAS INVOLVED IN A BIG FOOD FIGHT?

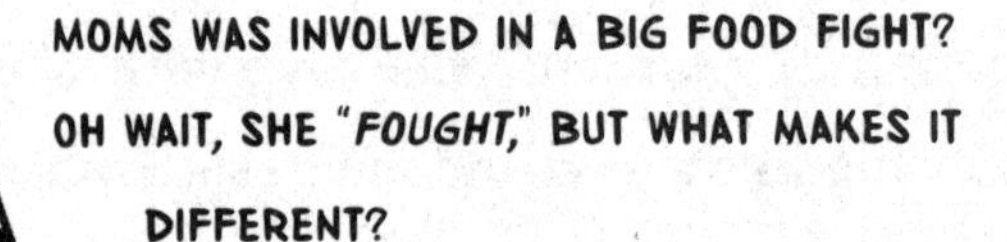

OH WAIT, SHE "*FOUGHT*," BUT WHAT MAKES IT DIFFERENT?
WEREN'T PEOPLE OUT THERE PUNCHIN' AND KICKIN'?

VEGGIES ARE COOL, BUT ARE THEY WORTH THE PROBLEMS?
COULDN'T FOLKS JUST TALK, USE WORDS TO SOLVE 'EM?
WHY THEY GOTTA FIGHT OVER CARROTS AND BEANS?
AND WHY WAS *MY* MAMA OUT THERE MAKING A SCENE?

I NEVER WOULDA THOUGHT MOMS HAD THAT FIRE

BUT I GUESS NOT HAVIN' PEAS MAKES YOU A FIGHTER!

NOW I KNOW WHY EVERYBODY'S PARENTS HATE...

...WHEN KIDS DON'T EAT THE VEGETABLES ON THEIR PLATE!

"Well, what did you do *then*?" She sprinkles the adobo bottle over the bowl of mashed potatoes and adds milk, garlic, and some shredded cheese. Moms never measures anything and somehow it still always tastes good. It's wild to think a lot of our food came from the ground on the next street. She turns her back to scoop the mashed potatoes back into the pot on the stove right when Dad brings me the Ziploc bag full of battered catfish and tells me, "Shake it." When I'm done, they trade places and Dad bops to a spot behind her where the hot oil is waiting for him in the frying pan. He must have switched over to his old-school jams, judging by the way he isn't laughing anymore and is off-key humming every few minutes. The first piece splashes and sizzles, and the smell of fried fish makes me think of that night in the park delivering dinner to Sunny.

"Simon, listen to me. It sounds to me like your school is doing the same thing that they did to our community back then. They're treating the after-school arts programs like they're not important. The same way we didn't let the Chicago City Council sleep until they did right by Creighton Park is the same way you can help your friend fight them taking away y'all's funding." Moms is saying so much at the same time. She's telling me to help Maria by fighting. She's saying stuff about funding. How are we supposed to do anything about all this? We're just kids. Who is Them? "And I'll find out who's on the school board, okay?" The School Board.

Aaron walks into the kitchen from his room and sneaks a scoop of Moms' mashed potatoes straight from the pot while she's still leaned over the counter staring at me. I catch Dad winking at him as he comes around the corner to mess with my things. He lifts up the picture Mr. James gave me. Right, homework. Ugh, almost forgot. He stares at it for a while and looks down at me.

"No justice, no peace." And he keeps his fist in the air until me, Moms, and Dad are all looking.

WEDNESDAY

CHAPTER 6

IF YOU DIDN'T ALREADY KNOW THIS WAS A classroom you might think it was a landfill. But for clothes. And it sort of smells a little bit like it, too, even though all these clothes are supposed to be clean. Must be a mix of smells of all the houses they came from. Maria steps out from behind the huge pants pile, raises a pair of jeans above her head, and disappears behind it. Me and C.J. crack up at this corny magic trick she's been doing like every five minutes as we sort through all the donations for students in need. Mr. James is the only teacher at Booker T. who eats cafeteria pizza, and he scarfs down a slice while he reads a book at his desk while Maria makes a big deal about how many Marias could fit in random pairs of pants.

"Yo, Deijah be wearing stuff like this," C.J. says, holding up an extra-small T-shirt with a giant unicorn that has a glittery rainbow over its horn. *Bars.*

"Oh das CUTE!" Maria squeals.

C.J. carefully folds the shirt the way Mr. James used a piece of cardboard to teach us how they do it at clothes stores. He puts it on top of a neat pile he has on one of the desks he's using just like the rest of us are doing. Maria's got pants, C.J.'s got shirts, and I've got dresses and jumpers. A few other kids have socks and shoes in the back of the room. This is our second time on donation duty since our first open mic at the shelter when I did the project on my friend Mr. Sunny. After the first one we had, people started bringing so much kids' clothes to the school that Mr. James had to get an even bigger cabinet than the one he had before and he set up a way for groups of kids to help sort everything during lunch a few times a week. When it's our turn, Mr. James lets us leave fifth period a little early so we can eat fast and come back to his room to help. We love doing this, low-key, cuz it feels like getting an extra recess and there aren't any Bobbys or Kennys in sight. Plus, Mr. James be playin' all the bops.

"Guys, I know what we can do," Maria says in a softer voice than usual. She takes a quick look over her shoulder at Mr. James to see if he's paying attention. He takes a huge gulp of orange pop and burps. Nope, not paying attention to us at all. She walks over to my pile with a pair of pants in her hands and pretends to fold, just in case.

"About what?"

She gives me a look that says *Really?*

"Oh, oh, oh, right. About who we about to fight, right, right," I say, trying to sound like I already understand.

"What y'all over here whispering about?" C.J. can never be left out of the action for too long. He walks over, folding a Chicago Bulls jersey that he'd probably beg Mr. James for if it was another two sizes bigger.

"I have an idea for how we can get our school's money back."

"Somebody stole the—"

Maria puts her face into her palm.

"Sssshhhhhh," I tell C.J., looking over his shoulder to make sure Mr. James is still in La La Land.

"A petition."

"Oh yeah! We could—wait, what's that again?"

I quickly realize I don't know that word. Or at least, I don't remember.

"Swear, I'm the only person who listens in class around here," Maria tells us, shaking her head. "It's what Mr. James talked about yesterday. It's something we can get people to sign to show the principal that a lot of people think it was wrong for them to take away our clubs."

SEE, I BE FORGETTIN', WHAT WAS A PETITION?
OH YEAH! SOMETHING TO MAKE PEOPLE LISTEN!
MR. JAMES SAYS IT ALWAYS STARTS WITH A VISION!

OR BETTER YET, A MISSION, WHEN THINGS NEED SOME FIXIN'.

YOU WANT FOLKS TO LISTEN? START A PETITION!
GET THEIR ATTENTION WITH THE STUFF THAT YOU MENTION!
GET THEM FIRED UP LIKE SMOKE IN AN ENGINE.
GET THEM FIRED UP LIKE THE STOVE IN A KITCHEN.
PETITION, PETITION! WE NEED A PETITION!
DON'T NEED A PHYSICIAN, DON'T NEED A MAGICIAN.

DON'T NEED MORE EXCUSES, OR STUFF TO BE MISSIN'.
WE NEED TO DO SOMETHING! PETITION, PETITION!

"Aw SNAP! Wait. How we gonna do that?" C.J. asks us both. He gets a pass cuz he's not in our class and Mrs. Leary definitely isn't the same kind of teacher ours is.

"I'll explain later, but last night my mama told me about how her and Auntie Julia stopped the city from putting another liquor store down the street from your house, C.J.," I say. C.J. looks up with a face that's less confused and a little more interested in what else Maria might say about petitions. I lean in a little more, too. Yesterday Maria said she wanted us to *fight* what's happening in our school and then Moms told me it's what her and Maria's mom did so we could have fresh vegetables in our neighborhood.

Maria says, "If we can get Ms. Berry to see that a lot of people in Creighton Park want us to have after-school programs, then maybe she could tell the school board that taking them away was a bad idea."

Mr. James clears his throat. We look in his direction and scatter back to our spots, realizing he's staring at us. Usually we wouldn't do this cuz Mr. James is chill during lunchtime, but the way Maria was talkin' made us all feel like it's something he's not supposed to know about even though it's something he taught us. A lot of things I overhear grown-ups talking about feel that way.

Maria looks up at the clock. Me and C.J. look and see we only have five more minutes left before recess. She looks back at us, poking her head out from behind her pile of clothes.

"Swings at recess." Our leader has a plan.

FRIDAY

CHAPTER 7

PICTURE THIS: ONE MAJORLY TALL MUS-cular dude leaned up against a dusty old red pickup truck. He's blasting jazz music, wearing a messed-up white jumpsuit, looking like he never really combs his hair but washes it with the fanciest shampoo. Then picture him with a toothpick sticking out the side of his mouth and super-dark sunglasses on. And if you need some help still, imagine Zion Williamson without the Pelicans jersey and all the sweat. Jumble all that up and you would come super close to C.J.'s dad, Uncle Jamaal. Besides their hair, they look almost exactly alike in the face, dark brown skin, goofy smile, and all. That's how he looks when he picks us up to start executing Maria's plan today.

"Go on 'head and squeeze up in there. Y'all ain't too old to rub elbows," he says while each of us climbs into his truck after school. C.J. climbs up first to sit next to his dad in the middle while me and Maria squeeze into the passenger seat. Uncle Jamaal always has a bunch of half-empty paint cans and heavy tool kits in the far back part so he only let us sit in there while he was driving once this summer after the beach. *I can't have y'all draggin' all them sea urchins and sand up in my convertible, now. Y'all can dry off in the back.* Don't nobody in Creighton Park drive a *real* convertible and I'm pretty sure nobody ever sees real sea urchins at the beach in the Chi. Just like C.J., Uncle Jamaal lives in a whole different world sometimes.

It only took about five seconds while he walked around to the driver's side for us to know what we were having for dinner tonight by the smell coming from the big white bag he put on C.J.'s lap. Just before he shut our door he told us not to touch nothin' till we get in the house. All three of us lick our lips knowing the white bag is packed with everything we love from Westside Wings & Barbecue. The empty space in my belly does backflips while I pass the seat belt across my chest, over Maria, to C.J. to lock it in. Moms always says if we don't wear our seat belts we'll fly through the car window, and Aaron says she's kidding, but I'm never laughing. I seen it on a cartoon once, so I know it could happen in real life. Uncle Jamaal flings his door open and jumps in just as C.J. tries to sneak a fry.

"Boy, I wasn't born yesterday. Get them non-bill-payin' hands out my food." Parents always call it their food cuz they paid for it. They have a point, but still. Uncle Jamaal is trippin' if he thinks we believe he's keeping it all to himself. That would not be cool.

The smell of barbecue mixes with the strawberry pine tree car freshener that's always dangling from Uncle Jamaal's rearview mirror on the short ride to C.J.'s. Ever since we've been at Booker T., C.J.'s only gotten to walk to school with me and

Maria a few times and that was when he slept over. He lives a little too far for all that. We drive down Linden, pass the shelter, and slow down for a yellow light at Claude. Right on the corner I see a small field that looks a little like a farm that's been there forever. This time I feel like I'm really seeing the small green sign on a wooden fence near the sidewalk for the first time: CREIGHTON COMMUNITY GARDEN. It's so little that I guess I never really cared what it said before. Plus, I never knew where Moms went for all the groceries. It sorta always feels like all our groceries magically appear every week.

We pass it in seconds like what I saw wasn't even real. It didn't look like it fit our hood surrounded by all these brick buildings but it was there just like Moms said. If Moms and Auntie Julia never said nothin' it'd probably be just another corner store with too many sale posters in the windows with the word LIQUOR hanging over the door in bright lights.

The light turns green and we make a left one block down on Cory Street where C.J. lives. We pull up to his house at the end of the block, and

C.J. climbs out of the truck behind his dad the second he unclicks the seat belt we all shared. He's up the front steps and turning the key while me and Maria barely have our door shut behind us. Barbecue is important biz. Ain't no time to waste when the grub is getting cold. My best friend knows what's up. Maria is the second person to get in the door and always the first one to get into the bathroom so she can wash her hands. If it wasn't for her, both me and C.J. would probably have a thousand diseases, I'm sure. Uncle Jamaal waits till I make it inside before he closes and locks the front door behind us.

The first time I went over to C.J.'s house I was surprised that he and his family are the only people that live in this building. Once you go up the steps and walk in the front door, we're in a whole house with two floors and a real backyard. There's pictures all over the walls in the dark hallway that's on the way to the bathroom and the living room, and everybody takes off their shoes right inside the front door along the carpet that leads to the kitchen. How many times has C.J. been saved by this bathroom? How many times did he get home from school with cafeteria-food bubble guts, glad the bathroom was right there? Probably too many to think about right now. Especially since we're about to eat.

Deijah already has all her *My Little Pony* folders, some work sheets, and color pencils spread all over the floor in the living room so we already know we'll have to work on our petition stuff somewhere else. Homework is basically coloring, measuring shapes, and sounding out every word aloud when you're in kindergarten. The good old days. Deijah's living the life. At the end of the hall, I can see C.J. already in the kitchen pulling everything out of the white bag as Maria comes out of the bathroom smelling like vanilla. One time C.J. told me Deijah gets to pick what hand soap they use in the front bathroom, so our hands always end up smelling like cakes and candy when we're at their house. Don't tell nobody but I kind of like it.

Nobody talks at the kitchen table. Not cuz it's rude or nothin' but because we're busy: Covered in three types of wings, slices of bread wrapped in napkins, two baskets of fries, and four pops, the kitchen counter is the Friday night of my dreams. All of a sudden it feels like summer again and we're at somebody's cookout stuffing our bellies till we can't move no more. The difference is Uncle Jamaal only bought enough for us all to get full, but not too much so we don't fall asleep. We got work to do. Before we can finish, he reminds us.

"All right, I told your mamas that I'm not gon' have y'all here all night. And I only gave you pop so you'll stay alert," he says, winking at me and Maria. "So get busy. Don't make me have to tell y'all to clean up, neither." We all scarf down the rest of our wings, adding to the pile of bones we put on a plate at the middle of the counter, and sip on orange, purple, and red pops while we start talking about our plans. Uncle Jamaal goes upstairs and we hear Deijah cut on the TV. It booms different voices and sound effects as she flips channels.

"Okay, so Mr. James says we have to get a lot! Like everybody gotta sign their name on it," Maria says while wiping a ring of honey barbecue sauce from around her mouth.

"And he said we need to tell people what they're signing up for," I add.

"Well, they're not signing up for anything. They're signing it to say they feel the same way as us."

"And what do we believe again?" C.J. asks, looking up from a napkin he's doodling on. Both me and Maria learned a long time ago that he's one of those kids that needs to doodle to stay focused. He used to get in trouble all the time cuz his old teachers thought he wasn't paying attention in class. He would get all these bad marks on his report card on the part where they say if we're good in class or not. Then Uncle Jamaal went up to Booker T. to meet with C.J.'s teacher and he never got a bad mark for participation ever again. I remember C.J. saying he was confused cuz he had good grades and everything. Now we know it's just how his brain works. Uncle Jamaal told C.J. that some teachers don't know that we all learn different.

"We believe that the school shouldn't take away all the money for after-school clubs. We believe that the school should use money for things we really need," Maria tells him, her voice all serious and loud.

C.J. raises his hands in the air like he's giving up. "Just a question."

"So we tell people what happened and get them to sign their name to our list and that's it?" I ask. This sounds too simple.

"Sort of," Maria says, reaching into her backpack. She pulls out two plain notebooks and drops them on the kitchen counter. "We can write down that we want our school clubs to have funding and then ask people to sign their names on the paper if they agree. Then they put the date next to all of it," she says. Nothing else. She opens one of the notebooks—Maria is the only kid I know with extra notebooks laying around for fun or serious stuff like this—and pulls out a big black marker. She writes: HELP US GET OUR SCHOOL MONEY BACK PLEASE. Under it she explains our situation in her own words. I'm glad she didn't give me that job. Maria has better handwriting than me and C.J.

Maria starts to write the same thing on the other notebook, and my mind starts doing a lot. I wonder what's the difference between writing your name and signing your name. Then I remember it's

probably that squiggly version of their name that adults put on permission slips for field trips and whatnot. Then I wonder what kids will sign on that part and how adults learned to do the squiggly thing with their names. C.J.'s voice crashes through my brain and brings me back.

"Y'all remember my uncle Terrance, who be giving those long speeches about life and stuff at Thanksgiving?" he asks.

"Yeah," we say.

"Well, he's always playing chess at Ford Park."

"And?" C.J.'s thoughts are always so random that Maria sounds a little annoyed at him for bringing one of them up when we're supposed to be working on our petition.

"AND he always over there with all his old chess friends. They're always so nice and always asking me about my homework and what's going on at school when my pop takes me and Deijah over there."

"Okaaay?"

"We can go over there! That's a whole bunch of easy names on our list! Uncle Terrance and his friends will sign whatever we want," C.J. shouts. Then, whispering, "I know because one time he signed my field trip slip to go to the Southside Skate Center when my mama said I couldn't go." We gasp.

"OOO, I'M TELLIN'!" Deijah screams from the living room.

"Mannnn, hush! You ain't gon' do nothin'!" Sounds harsh but he's right. Deijah only makes threats so she can be in our business, but C.J. always reminds her that she's little and he's big and he ain't havin' it. Deijah doesn't say anything else and flips to another channel. "For real, y'all, we should go there first!"

"Plus, when people see some names on the list already, they gonna know we're serious!" Maria adds, finishing the message on the second notebook. Uncle Jamaal's feet coming down the stairs almost sound like somebody beating on the front door and my heart races for a second. I don't notice I'm holding my breath for a few seconds until I hear him telling Deijah she better have her homework done since the TV's on. A strong breeze of soap, cocoa butter, and baby powder floats toward us when he walks past us to open the fridge.

"Uuuuugh! Ain't nothin' good on!"

"Got a whole iPad and more toys than Walmart and got the nerve to complain," Uncle Jamaal says to the water bottle he twists open. Sometimes I'm surprised that Deijah and C.J. have stuff like iPads cuz the rest of their house seems kind of old-fashioned. Like who still has cable? And the furniture? Only difference between theirs and Grandma Lucille's is they don't still got the plastic cover on the couch. Uncle Jamaal shakes his head after he drinks most of his water, laughs at whatever's in his head, and goes back to the living room. The channels flip for a few seconds more.

BUY ONE GET ONE FR—

LAST WEEK ON HOAR—

AT TWO THIRTY THIS AFTERNOON A GROUP—

COACH DOC RIVERS HAS CA—

"Hold up, baby girl, run that back. Let me see something," Uncle Jamaal tells Deijah.

"Daddy, I don't wanna watch that!" A few minutes later, Deijah stomps all the way upstairs with her backpack and slams the door. Uncle Jamaal flips back to the Channel 7 news. *"Thank you, Mark, yes, following yesterday's verdict a group of protesters have reportedly had their hands locked in what looks like a human chain across I-94 since two thirty this afternoon. Traffic is backed up all the way to…"* I stop being able to hear the reporter's voice on the TV when C.J. starts crumpling up all our food bags and throwing stuff in the trash.

Uncle Jamaal starts going off at the TV. "It don't make no dang sense! These kids get mad and then make life hard for everybody! Don't nobody got time for all that. We saw the same things goin' on when we was kids and you don't see us out here beggin' and cryin' and carryin' on about it. A lot of them probably couldn't even tell you what they mad about. Kids these…" His voice sort of starts to sound far away but I can't stop thinking about what the reporter said. A whole bunch of people on the South Side made people late to where they were going. Nobody could drive past I-94 because they wouldn't get out of the street, just like the people in the picture Mr. James showed us on Monday. Now they're on the news.

NO JUSTICE, NO PEACE! NO JUSTICE, NO PEACE!
IS THIS THE REASON WHY THERE'S PEOPLE LINED
UP IN THE STREETS?
AARON SAID THAT TO ME WITH A FIST UP IN THE
SKY

AND NOW THESE FOLKS ON TV ARE NOT LETTING
PEOPLE BY.

NO JUSTICE, NO PEACE! NO JUSTICE, NO PEACE!
IT'S GOT ME THINKIN' 'BOUT THOSE PROTESTERS
IN THE STREET.

THEY HAD A PILLOW, AND THEY WERE
PRETENDING TO BE 'SLEEP.
PLUS, I THINK IT WAS ABOUT BREONNA AND
POLICE.

NO JUSTICE, NO PEACE! NO JUSTICE, NO PEACE!
I FEEL THIS PROTESTING GIVES A LOT OF PEOPLE
GRIEF.
C.J.'S DAD SAYS "PROTESTING ISN'T RIGHT!"
BUT MR. JAMES SAYS "PROTESTING IS A RIGHT!"

MOMS SAYS SHE FOUGHT! MARIA WANTS TO
FIGHT!
C.J.'S DOWN FOR ANYTHING, AND ME? I THINK I
MIGHT!
MAYBE I'MA JUST HAVE TO STAND ON MY
BELIEFS!

NO JUSTICE, NO PEACE! NO JUSTICE, NO PEACE!

"Helloooooo. Earth to Siiiimon!" I shake my head and realize Maria has her hands on my shoulders, shaking me out of my daydream. "It's time to go. Auntie Sharon is back from work and she said we better get in the car before she gets comfy."

"Let's go, y'all," Auntie Sharon orders from the front hallway. She still has on her salon shirt and work shoes, which are just some rubber slides with holes in them. After Auntie Sharon got her own spot in the back of Mr. Ray's barbershop braiding hair, we haven't really seen her wear anything else. I hop down off the kitchen stool and throw my backpack on to meet Maria at the front door. While we put on our shoes Auntie Sharon leans over the couch and kisses Uncle Jamaal on his cheek. I pretend to gag when me and Maria look at each other, and she tells me to grow up.

Auntie Sharon turns back around, flinging all her braids off her shoulder, and we get a whiff of burnt hair, grease, and the spray Mr. Ray uses on us after a haircut. The oily stuff, not the stuff that makes your scalp feel like it's frying.

Uncle Jamaal mumbles some other stuff at the TV on our way out.

"This ain't the way to do it. This ain't the way to get things done," I hear him say. "Look at 'em! Couldn't be more than twenty of them out there.

They doin' all this and it's only twenty folks. Does anybody even know their demands? Exactly," he says, answering his own question. "Ain't nobody gon' care." Demands.

Auntie Sharon pulls the door shut behind us.

SATURDAY

CHAPTER 8

MY ALARM CLOCK BARELY BUZZES TWO times before I slam the snooze button with the palm of my hand and climb back across my blanket to the edge of my bed closest to the door. My chin slams hard into the floor while my feet fly over my head and down to the rug, leaving me flipped over flat, facing the ceiling. I squint across our dark room, checking to see if anybody witnessed it, and DeShawn pokes his head out from under his covers, shakes his head, and goes back to sleep. Markus doesn't even move. Saturday is the day they try to pretend they don't have any responsibilities. I wake up with one responsibility that's too important to sleep on. I fling the door open and run down the hall, hearing Dad shuffling around in the kitchen even though I don't smell nothin' breakfasty happenin' in there.

"Where y'all going?" I blurt out the minute I realize both my parents are heading toward the front door. Out of breath and feeling like I have to talk fast, I don't have time to say anything else.

"Well, good morning to you, too, Simon," Moms says, looking over her shoulder, gasping for a second when she checks out what I just did to my face. Both of her shoulders have bags full of kitchen tools and groceries, otherwise a whole first aid kit woulda been out already. Her eyes watch the blood starting to ooze from my chin.

"How'd you sleep, little ma—I mean, Notorious D.O.G.?" I can tell by the way Dad says this that he's tryna soften me up. He's got more grocery bags in both hands. He steps closer to get a better look at the open cut I just gave myself rushing out of bed and drops the bags in front of the door.

"I slept fine. Y'all about to leave? We're getting

people to sign our petition today!" I coulda sworn I told Dad about the plan last night when I got back from C.J.'s, and I even mentioned it to Moms that night right after Maria told us what she was thinking at lunch. And when I got back home last night I still had to make something else for Maria so I couldn't talk too much before bed. But they still should have remembered. Maybe they're just running to the store for breakfast stuff. Yeah, that's it. *Chill, Simon.* They both look at each other for a second before Moms starts to answer and Dad starts to move.

"Simon, baby, you know I made a commitment at the shelter, right?" She pauses, waiting for me to say something about how she promised to cook at the shelter a few Saturdays a month. "Baby, you don't think you need a Band-Aid or somethin'?"

"And I'm picking up your friend Sunny. Gonna take him for a haircut and a shave. Gonna give him some time to get himself cleaned up and in some new clothes that don't smell like the shelter. We thought it'd be good for us to do this on the same day. Plus, it'll give us a head start on making sure things are all set for your open mic tomorrow. You know how it is over there, Si. They forget we're comin' sometimes. Here, let me just..." Dad is tryna back Moms up so I don't get too mad about what they're not really telling me. He seems like it only takes him four steps, tops, to get in and out of the kitchen with a wet towel. He grabs my head and pushes my chin in it and the coldness spreads through my face. We hear the toilet flush from down the hall and Aaron lets out a dramatic yawn as he flings the door open. He scratches his stomach, walking through the kitchen into the living room, and plops down onto the couch.

"Don't nobody go in there for at least thirty to forty-five minutes," he says, laughing by himself. He takes a look at the three of us and pulls his phone from the pocket of his basketball shorts.

"Like I was saying," Moms continues while clearing her throat. "We made a commitment at the shelter to keep helping after your project was over, and we need to do what we said we're gonna do. Including being here for our family so we can help others," she adds, eyeballing Aaron and pausing for a second. His thumb is already in scrolling position, and his mouth hangs open a little bit as his thumb sweeps the screen upward, over and over again. He double-taps and then keeps going. At this rate, Moms will never let me get my own cell phone. If you cracked open Aaron's skull, you'd prob find nothing but mush up in there. "When one of us cares about something important in this house, we all care about it," Moms says. "That's why Aaron agreed to take you and your friends out to get people to sign y'all's petition today."

Aaron's thumb freezes and he stares in the direction of his phone for a second but is clearly no longer scrolling. I know he has no idea how helping me with this petition stuff has anything to do with him. But Moms don't sound like she's asking. He looks like he's about to say something to her but instead he lets out a deep sigh, dropping his phone into his lap and folding his arms. Whatever he was about to waste his Saturday on just got cut by Moms' deathly stare. Sometimes Aaron looks like wherever he puts all his quick comebacks and anger toward grown-ups is going to get too big to stay inside him. One day, it's all gonna come spraying out like Silly String from the can, water hose style.

"Okay, okay, you got it, Ma," Aaron says in a way that sorta sounds like he just wants Moms to leave him alone. *You got it* is definitely code for *STOP TALKING.* And it really sounds like a polite way to tell Moms to stop talking without getting grounded. He might not care about what me, C.J., and Maria got going on but if agreeing to chaperone us today means Moms will get off his back, Aaron will probably do it.

"Why don't you take 'em up over on Linden to that block party they got goin' on today after y'all leave Ford Park. It's beautiful out and it's gon' be plenty of people out there, jammin' and eatin' and whatnot. It'll be easy, son." Now it sounds like Dad is talking to both of us. "Besides, I know you and your boys was probably gonna end up over there later anyway." Dad opens the front door and steps back to let Moms walk out first and uses his head to call Aaron over to him. He lowers his voice and reaches out to shake Aaron's hand while leaning in to speak into his ear: "Just think of it as a paid vacation." I catch a flash of green and white going in between their hands.

He palms Aaron's head like a basketball, pulling him in to kiss his forehead, pushes him back away from the door, and tells me to get a Band-Aid from the cabinet above the refrigerator. Then they're both gone. Aaron raises the twenty-dollar bill in the air the way they check to see if it's real at the movies and speaks to me for the first time since walking into the living room.

"You're on your own, fool. I'm eating good today. Better get you some cereal and get dressed before I change my mind."

☆ ☆ ☆

Getting up early enough to make it into the bathroom before DeShawn and Markus is worth finding out that Aaron is taking us to get signatures instead of our parents. I got enough time to figure out my look before anybody starts banging on the door for me to hurry up. Everybody always needs the bathroom at the same time in the morning and I need to be far away from here when all that starts to go down. I try on three looks before I settle on one of my favorite *Black Panther* T-shirts with M'Baku on the front, a pair of khaki cargo pants with lots of pockets, and a pair of Jordans that Grandma Lucille got me last year even though Moms said I don't need no expensive sneakers. Granny said she *don't have nothin' to do with my money no way.* I stare at myself in the mirror while using Markus's brush to smooth down my sideburns and think about the different pictures Mr. James showed us this week. I don't look nothin' like the people he told us were in the original Black Panther Party. They wore black head to toe all the time but I just look like me.

I SAW PICTURES OF FRED HAMPTON AND HUEY
NEWTON,
SOME ACTIVISTS FROM WAY BACK, NOT BOOKER
T. STUDENTS.

THE WAY THEY WERE DRESSED SHOWS ME THEY
MEANT BUSINESS.

ALL BLACK—THAT'S WHAT YOU 'SPOSE TO WEAR,
ISN'T IT?

BUT HONESTLY, I SEEN OTHER PEOPLE DO IT
DIFFERENT.

AND WEARING WHAT *THEY* WANT NEVER MESSED
UP *THEIR* MISSION.
BEYONCÉ SPEAKS UP WHEN SHE WEARS IVY PARK,
AND A WOMAN NAMED MALALA WEARS A COOL
HEAD SCARF!

MARI COPENY, SHE'S A KID LIKE ME
WHO WAS DRESSED IN SOME JEANS AND A PLAIN
OL' TEE.
DON'T FORGET LEBRON JAMES (HE RELATED TO
MY TEACHER?).
ANYWAYS...HE WEARS A JERSEY, OR A SUIT, OR
SNEAKERS.

SO I GUESS AN ACTIVIST CAN REALLY DRESS HOW
THEY LIKE
JUST AS LONG AS THEY'RE READY TO PUT UP A
GOOD FIGHT!
TO SCRAP, TO RUMBLE, TO WRESTLE, TO SPAR--
NOT ABOUT WHAT YOU WEAR, IT'S ABOUT WHO
YOU ARE.
WOOF! WOOF!

The doorbell rings and I know it has to be Maria.

"OH EM GEE, SIMON! I'm SO excited!" Maria starts talking a hundred miles a minute about all the places we could go before she's all the way in the door. Her big sister, Camille, walks in behind her, looking like she feels the same way Aaron does. When she sits down on the couch and pulls out her phone I know she probably got the same speech, too, since Ms. Estelle doesn't walk through the door behind them. I don't see Maria and Camille together that much cuz Camille is always hanging out with her middle-school friends or blasting somebody named Noname in her room for hours. But when I do, I remember how different they are. From her skin to her clothes to her hair, I'd never think Camille was Maria's big sister if I saw her walking down the street and didn't already know who she is. Today Maria's neon-yellow frames match some of the stripes in her favorite T-shirt that matches the patches in her favorite pair of jeans that match the shoelaces on her favorite pair of Vans. Her Afro puffs look especially tight next to the big, loose chunky curls hanging out of the opening of Camille's black hoodie. Camille pulls the strings of her hood even tighter so the curls almost cover her face and slouches deeper into the couch. Me and Maria can hear the music blasting from her earbuds all of a sudden so it's not surprising when she stuffs both her hands into the pouch of her overalls, leans back, and closes her eyes.

Maria hands over a map that she drew last night of all the stops we can make today. Whoa. "Simon, we can get HUNDREDS of signatures if we go here, here, here, and here and...," she says pointing to each place that I hadn't even thought about.

The doorbell starts ringing over and over, drowning out Maria's travel plans. C.J.'s drip isn't a surprise but it's never not funny when any kind of important day comes around. To start with: Homie's haircut is so fresh it looks like he walked out of Mr. Ray's five minutes ago. Forehead so shiny I probably could brush my teeth in it. I cough the second I open the door wide enough to let him in and a

big gust of too much of Uncle Jamaal's cologne busts me in the face.

"Who's in charge here?" is how Auntie Sharon says hello to me, stepping halfway in the door and peering around it to search our apartment for a grown-up. By this time, C.J.'s checking himself out in the big mirror by the door, not paying attention to me and Maria trying to hide how hard we both want to laugh.

Aaron walks through the kitchen, dressed and durag-less, with DeShawn and Markus behind him, and it looks like he used his big brother powers to transfer however he was feeling earlier over to them, which means he's making them go with us, too. Both of them drag their feet behind him, pulling on wrinkled T-shirts and pushing crust out their eyes until they get one look at C.J. They lose it, and in seconds, Markus has tears streaming down his face from laughing so hard. I cover my mouth with one hand and point at Aaron with the other to answer Auntie Sharon's question.

She sizes him up and I guess how big he is makes her believe me. When her eyes reach the top of his head, way above hers, she tells C.J., "That money I gave you is for the whole day, so don't go blowin' it all in one place," in the same voice Dad used earlier to Aaron.

I stop laughing when I realize Dad left any money I might need in Aaron's pocket. Face-palm.

"Preach, PreaCHA!" DeShawn hollers, crashing into Markus. He takes off running into the kitchen with one hand in the air and runs back with a dish-rag, waving it like one of the old church ladies yelling things out during the sermon on Sundays.

"Boy, ya look like you 'bouta collect offering! Ha! That boy so fresh and so clean! Ha!" Markus shouts like the preaching pastor DeShawn's talking to. I can tell by the look on Auntie Sharon's face before she shuts the door behind her that the whole situation is way too dramatic but I catch C.J. cracking a smile, too. He's been wearing suits for special days since I met him in kindergarten and all the other times they laughed didn't stop him. Aaron shakes C.J.'s hand, bending down to straighten the tie that he'd been trying to fix in the mirror. C.J. turns to face Aaron for help with his collar and slaps Aaron's hand away the second he notices somebody's on the far end of the couch.

Camille had her eyes closed all the way up until Markus started going off about C.J.'s look. She pulls her hands out of her overalls, turns off whatever's blasting in her earbuds, and pulls her hood all the way off.

"I got this," C.J. tells Aaron with his eyes stuck on Camille.

"Can we go or what? I got homework," she says, paying my boy no attention at all.

"Who's pressed to get back home to do *work*?" DeShawn says, nudging Markus like Camille is some type of joke.

"We are." And Maria walks to the door and waits while we all rush to get ready to go.

CHAPTER 9

THE L TRAIN SCREECHES TO A LOUD STOP over our heads as we walk into the entrance of Ford Park, a fifteen-minute walk outside Creighton. C.J. barely has to tell us where to find his uncle Terrance and friends: We follow the voices of a bunch of old dudes arguing about one time, back in the day, when one of them stole somebody else's girl. Through the short trees and wide bushes, we all walk down a short path that leads to where all the chess tables are set up under a huge arch. Their voices turn into loud echoes around us right as we see them.

"Now you know you a lie, Garold. Bernice was sweet on me before she ever even knew you existed, brotha!"

"Is *that* what she told you? Oh please. *I* was the only gentleman in all of Booker T. who walked Bernice to school *Every. Single. Day.* Ain't none of y'all know nothin' about chivalry. I ain't have to steal her, my man. She was already mine!"

"But who did she let carry her books, though?" I recognize Uncle Terrance super quick by the way C.J. always describes him. A picked-out gray Afro stuffed under a large black cowboy hat. Check. Shiny brown skin with holes all over his face that look like freckles until you get up close. Check. An oversized T-shirt of some band we've never heard of that looks like he wears it every day. Tucked in. Check, check. Jeans pulled up high on his waist. Check. Sneakers that look kind of cool but also like they're from the eighties. Check. A big booming laugh that sounds like he's wheezing and a smooth, warm voice that can break up any fight before it gets out of control. Check, check. He high-fives into a handshake with a dude who's sitting across from him looking like he sprayed his hair color on. Uncle Terrance looks like you could never tell where he's from or where he's going. I'd never EVER be caught in Booker T. looking like *that*. Maybe he's too old to care but not even Grandma Lucille be lookin' that wild. It's kind of cool that he's not worried about what people see when they look at him.

UNCLE T, UNCLE TERRANCE,
KINDA WEIRD, THAT'S APPARENT.
UNIQUE STYLE, MAYBE SO!
LOW--KEY KINDA BRAZY, THO!
NOT GON' WIN NO FASHION SHOWS
DRESSED LIKE THIS, AND THAT'S FASHO!
BUT HE'S KINDA SWAGGY STILL,
CONFIDENT, AND THAT'S FOR REAL.
UNCLE T, UNCLE TERRANCE,
KINDA WEIRD, THAT'S APPARENT.

"Aw SOOKY, SOOKY, now! If it ain't MY MAN: Baby Obama! *THE CHANGE WE NEED! Ha haaaaaa!*" Uncle Terrance starts up when C.J. reaches their table first. The fact that C.J.'s drowning in his infamous light brown church suit doesn't help the nickname. All his friends add their two cents:

"Okay! That boy SHAWP, do you hear me? Lookin' like Pastor Mike on Easter Sunday after the collection plate done got filled up!"

"Lookin' like one of them Nation of Islam brothers who be sellin' them bean pies and newspapers over by the freeway!"

"Lookin' *smoove* as a bowl of grits!"

"Lookin' like a whole lotta money! Check you out, little man. Out here on a Saturday doin' big thangs, huh?" Uncle Terrance brings it all the way home with the last compliment while C.J. just stands there sweating under the sun, only wiping at his greasy forehead once. Uncle Terrance pulls C.J. into a hug so big it looks like it hurts a little.

"C'mon, Uncle T, you gon' wrinkle my best shirt," C.J. tells him, pushing back and brushing his suit jacket down with both hands. After he's quiet for a few seconds the table notices the rest of us all of a sudden and C.J. gets a break. It feels like old folks are the same no matter where you go. They all wanna do math equations about your body and make such a big deal about how big you've grown since the last time they saw you. Even if they just saw you last week. Every time I see Grandma Lucille I get ready to hear her talking about how many diapers of mine she's changed and how it'll be time for me to learn to drive and get married soon. The Notorious D.O.G. is big and all but *whoa.* While they each go down the line of us, gassing up DeShawn's fade, Marcus's sneakers, and Aaron's computer-sized phone, I see Maria squat down behind everybody to pull out both of our notebooks for the signatures. Camille's hoodie is back over her head and she's sitting at the next table playing a game of chess by herself.

"I thought these might help a little," I say.

Maria looks into the pile of different-colored flyers in my hand, confused. We never talked about this. "Mr. James said we gotta tell people why we're doin' this, right?" Maria throws her arms around me and squeezes so hard, for a second I worry about last night's wings coming back up. Lemon pepper chicken chunks. I can already feel the burn in the back of my throat. *Gurgle.* When she finally lets me go she stands next to me and flips through each of them. I take one copy back and she follows me while I read it out loud:

WE, THE SCHOLARS OF THE BOOKER T. SCHOOL,
DO HEREBY DECLARE THAT SOME THINGS AIN'T
COOL!

LIKE NOT GETTING MONEY FOR OUR CLUBS AND
OUR TEAMS.
IT DOESN'T MAKE SENSE, SO WE'RE TRYNA
CHANGE THINGS!
STUDENTS NEED PROGRAMS, IS WHAT THE
STUDIES SHOW,

SO WE GON' GET THEM BACK SO THAT KIDS CAN
GROW!
BUT WE NEED YOUR HELP, CAN'T DO IT BY
OURSELF.
DON'T GOTTA HAVE POWER OR A WHOLE LOTTA
WEALTH.

YOU JUST GOTTA SIGN YOUR NAME, THAT'S THE
PLAN.

JOIN US IF YOU CAN, CUZ WE'RE TAKING A
STAND!

"Oh em gee, Simon. These are so great! And I love how they rhyme. These will have great Impact, with a capital *I*, as my tio would say," Maria says. We both smile.

Over Maria's shoulder, I see everybody crowding Uncle Terrance's chess table even tighter, and C.J. waves both of us over. Uncle Terrance is in the middle of explaining chess when we get there.

"You see me and Clyde here got all the same sixteen pieces. Each of 'em get to do different thangs

but both of us start with all the same ones. How we win is in how we strategize, Mr. Prez." Uncle Terrance winks at C.J. even though he's talking to all of us now. He lightly jabs an elbow into C.J.'s side where a pit stain is already spreading from his underarms all the way down his side. Homie really chose the worst thing to wear to take a long walk on a Saturday that must have forgot it's fall and not still summer. "You see, real life ain't like chess. In life you got people over here with thirty-nine pieces and then people over there with twelve. Some people got both color pieces while others got none at all. I been playin' this game all my life waiting for the real world to feel like this board.

"Something that is a lot like life, though, is the way every chess game starts. The player with the white pieces always gets the first move. I know a thang or two about them people on the other side of town who always seem to get everything first. Cleaner streets. Nicer neighborhoods. Grocery stores with real food in 'em. Schools with new books and expensive technology all up in *every* classroom..."

"That's just like what my mama says," Maria tells him. "She said we deserve good stuff, too."

"That's right, baby girl. We fight because we don't all start out with the same pieces and some of us never get to throw the first punch." I bet Mr. James and Uncle Terrance could kick it. They both talk in code whenever they're in front of a group of kids. They both always got a goofy smile on their faces like they know something that the rest of the world doesn't know. "It ain't right. But chess teaches us what can happen when we all start out with the things we need to win." Maria hands him one of the flyers I made before I get a chance to stop her. I didn't really think about anybody else looking at them but her even though they were meant to be seen. "Wow, y'all official as a whistle, huh? That's all right."

"All y'all went to Booker T., too?" I have to make sure what I heard earlier was right.

"You made this, didn't you?" He answers me with a slight smirk. "Young'un over here is president material but he don't like to write too much. That's how I know *he* ain't do it. More of a sports man. You tryin' out for that there football this year, Cornelius?"

"Maybe basketball," C.J. forces himself to say through his teeth.

"Y-yeah, I made it." Hopefully he didn't hear me stutter. Grown folks always—

"You sure, son? You don't sound too sure." Grown folks always gotta point out your flaws. They can't ever just pretend they didn't see or hear that embarrassing thing you did.

"I made it." He shakes his head and chuckles at me trying to sound more confident. He reads the flyer again while Maria takes this as her cue to hand them the notebooks and pens.

"Do you agree with us, Mr. Terrance?" she asks him, shoving her notebook into his empty hand. "If you agree, then you can put your name riiiight here!"

"This a girl about her business, I see! That's what I'm talkin' about! That's all right," he says, still looking all over the flyer like it might have a secret door with something else hidden in it. He writes his name *TERRANCE REGINALD JONES* and squiggles his signature with a few lines and circles before passing it across the board to Clyde. By now the whole table has their own copies and Clyde looks at his like he's inspecting it, too. Uncle Terrance goes on, "We was runnin' up and down them school halls long before y'all was even born. I been around a long time and even though I keep seeing the same ol' stuff, some things been changing around here for the good 'cause of kids like y'all." He pauses for old-man dramatic effect, making eye contact with all of us. Even Camille, who's now hovering behind me. C.J.'s chest puffs out a little bit hearing this.

"*I* told them we needed to do this!"

"I'm sure you did, son. That's too bad what's happenin' over at y'all's school. Can't say it's anything new. I'm proud of you kids for making some more noise around here." My brain flashes back to those protesters on TV at C.J.'s house making a human chain. I hear them chanting Breonna Taylor's name and their demands in the background while the reporter talked over the angry horns of cars stuck in traffic because of them. *This ain't the way to do it.... They doin' all this and it's only twenty folks.... Ain't nobody gon' care.* Uncle Jamaal didn't sound like making noise was a good thing. I don't know what it means for him to be so upset with the people on TV standing up for what they believe in while Uncle Terrance, who's been around longer, is telling us he's proud. How can you tell what's the right thing when grown folks don't even know what to do?

Mr. Clyde picks up a piece I don't know the name of and replaces one of Uncle Terrance's pieces that I don't know the name of and Uncle Terrance's reaction makes the whole table explode. Imagine four old dudes who look like they got dressed in another time zone without mirrors suddenly screaming into each other's faces. They all laugh so loud you could probably hear it all the way on the other side of the park.

"Yooooooo, that was WIIILLLD!" Aaron says to Clyde while shaking his hand.

"What happened? What he do? He won the game?!" None of us is cool enough to pretend that long about knowing which move was pulled or what it means.

"Iono, I'm just ready to get out of here. You better act like you get it so these grandpas don't keep wrappin' us up, *young'un*. Pop ain't pay me enough for this." Aaron doesn't know what just happened on the chessboard, either. "It's Saturday, bruh. That better be the last speech we gotta sit through for the day." And it don't seem like he even cares.

That's all right.

CHAPTER 10

DAD MIGHT NOT HAVE PAID AARON ENOUGH to sit through speeches on a Saturday but he definitely paid him more than enough to kick it with all his high school friends at the Creighton Fall Back Block Party put on every year around the beginning of fall. That's basically what he tries to do when we get here. Altogether, it's seven of us, but the second we pass the entrance, Aaron acts like he's a party of one and like he don't know us. His favorite velvet durag magically reappears and he ties the bow closer to the front of his face this time. Two of his homies that's been over to our house a few times,

Rashad and Brandon, walk over to dap him up and he's almost gone until Maria—

"UM, EXCUSE ME?!" She blocks his way with her arms folded and taps her foot, making a little scene next to the ticket booth. Aaron tries to play it smooth in front of his friends but all the grown folks walking by, whispering how cute she is, ruin all his plans of escape. He's always tryna get rid of me and my friends when Moms forces him to watch us but our parents never believe me when I try to tell them.

"Aight, aight," he mumbles to Maria. "Yo, I'ma catch up with y'all later," he tells his friends.

"Bet," DeShawn and Markus say at the same time, taking that as their cue to escape, too. They run off in the same direction as Aaron's friends and leave him with us. Up until then I almost forgot they were here. Standing in Aaron's way would have never worked for me. Thanks to Maria, we get to keep Aaron for the short two blocks that the block party takes up along Linden Boulevard. Both ends of the street are blocked off by giant orange cones with every color balloon. The sides of the street are lined with almost everybody you need to know in Creighton Park and everything you want to do on a Saturday: all the food and games in the front and all the boring stuff, like park safety, in the back. Performances in the middle.

"Look, we gon' get y'all's business handled quick. I ain't got all day. In one hour we gon' meet back up at the main stage, aight?" I peer at the main stage out the corner of my eye, not wanting to check it out directly so no one gets any big ideas. It's too many people here for all that. Right now all that's onstage is a drum set, some loudspeakers, and a mic. When things really get started all these people will crowd around it and get super close to whoever's gon' be up there and I'm glad it ain't me. It's still early and people are too busy eating brats, deep-dish, Mexican corn, and wings, sitting on the curbs and scattered around the street, but when performances start, all their eyes will go up there. It's so much going on that it's almost too hard to imagine that cars drive through here on normal days, but today, it's a whole world by itself.

Maria opens her backpack and hands me the

notebook that she didn't take out at the park earlier. This the first time that I notice both covers look way different than last night. She's decked them out with a Maria version of graffiti and it's actually kinda cool. In big black letters, each cover says *PETITION FOR BOOKER T. WASHINGTON ELEMENTARY SCHOOL AFTER-SCHOOL CLUBS.* Before she lets go of mine, she waits for me to look her dead in her face.

"Guard this with your life, Simon." With my *LIFE*? Sheesh. "I'm serious. When we show Ms.

Berry that all these people want us to keep our clubs, she'll make the school board give our money back. So we can't mess this up."

OKAY, SIMON! DO EVERYONE A FAVOR.
DON'T MESS IT UP—NOT NOW, NOT LATER.
DO THIS THING RIGHT FOR THE GREAT DEBATER.
MARIA'S COUNTIN' ON YOU LIKE A CALCULATOR.
THE PRESSURE'S ON ME, BUT SEE, I CAN HANDLE.
JUST DON'T BLOW IT LIKE A BIRTHDAY CANDLE.
DON'T LOSE NOTHIN', THAT'LL BE A SCANDAL.
DON'T MESS IT UP, OR HER LIFE'S IN SHAMBLES.
I'MA GET IT RIGHT! IT'LL BE FINE.
I'MA GET FIFTY BILLION PEOPLE TO SIGN.
BUT WHAT IF THEY DON'T? IF NOBODY SIGNS IT?
WHAT IF I LOSE THE BOOK AND NOBODY FINDS IT?
OR WORSE, WHAT IF BOBBY TAKES IT AND HIDES IT?
I CAN'T DENY IT, I HATE SURPRISES!
IT COULD GO SO WRONG BECAUSE OF SILLY ME!
THEN WE WOULD LOSE EVERY CLUB AT BOOKER T.!

"I got you," I tell her, trying my best not to sound as nervous as I feel. Notorious D.O.G. ain't too good under pressure. I wrap my arms around the notebook dramatically the way I've seen girls hold things when they're feeling all googly-eyed about stuff. I've seen it in movies, so I know they do it. Maria just stares back at me. There isn't even a little giggle she's trying to hide. I remember the flyers. "What do you think we should do with these? I don't think I made enough."

"You made them to tell people what's happening at our school, right?"

Kind of. Also made them so I wouldn't really have to talk to these people. Same thing.

"Well...yeah."

"Then when you run out, that's all you gotta do, silly." *Tell people what's happening to our school.*

CHAPTER 11

THE FIRST THING AARON DOES WHEN OUR group splits up is buy a giant pretzel with part of the money Dad gave him this morning. None for me, of course. Through a mouth full of soggy bread and hot cheese he starts giving me game on how to get my notebook filled with signatures like it's a competition or something. He rubs his hands together to brush off all the salt and points to the best spots to go to first, telling me old folks and people who got kids will be the easiest. The plan: go to everybody sitting on benches and chairs first by myself while he watches. He says it's to give me space but I feel like he knows all the grandpas and grandmas will think I'm cuter by myself. Plus, he's still low-key salty that he's basically stuck with me on one of the funnest days to be on the West Side when he'd rather be kicking it with his friends. I go first to Mr. Ray, who's giving out free shape-ups for the day.

"Mr. Simon Barnes, my boy! What you got there?" I hold up one of the flyers so he can read while he clips a piece of paper around a customer's neck before taping the barber cape in place. "Booker T. Washington Elementary School…uh-huh… uh-huh…after-school clubs…uh-huh…mmmm… sign the petition…" He brushes the man's hair before he pauses. "Well, Mr. Barnes, you've got my vote! They always tryna take y'all's fun away, huh? Then they wonder why these young'uns around here keep getting into trouble. The kids ain't got nothin' to do, that's why! I tell ya…" I let Mr. Ray ramble about a bunch of stuff the way he does every time I'm in his chair. I start to tune him out once he gives the signed notebook back to me and he hands the flyer to his customer. Before I know it, everybody waiting in line to get shaped up by Mr. Ray signs our petition.

A lady sitting on a small chair next to a table full of oil pastels like the ones we used in art class once calls me over and tells me to sit in the chair across from her. I recognize her from the first one of these block parties I came to, and she reminds me her name is Ms. Tracy. That first year she drew a basketball on one side of my face because I told her I liked LeBron James. On the other side she drew music notes and a mic because Moms told her I could rap a little bit. Imagine it: a big ol' orange ball on one side and a microphone on the other. A whole mess.

"Rhymin' Simon! I knew that was you, boo. What you gettin' this time? Are you a big-time rapper yet?" You tell a grown-up that you rap ONE time and they make a big deal about it every time they see you after that. Ms. Tracy smiles up at me and winks. "Give me them papers. I know you too grown for this. Wouldn't be caught dead with face paint now, huh? Boy, I tell ya, y'all grow up so dang fast, got me checking my scalp for mo' gray hairs every day. I'm proud of you, baby boy," she says, handing the notebook and her flyer to the lady who's been ear hustling at the table next to us. "Some of us is tired of fighting. Now y'all out here takin' the reins! That's what *I'm* talkin' 'bout!"

This is how most of the hour walking around trying to get signatures goes. At first I take Aaron's advice and avoid all the kids. Grandparents, parents, and people I know, like Ms. Tracy and Mr. Ray only. But then we bump into C.J., Maria, and Camille on the other side of the street surrounded by kids.

"It's so easy, Simon. All the kids here go to Booker T. and they BIG mad just like us. And don't we need *everybody* to sign? Kids' signatures are probably worth DOUBLE the points, right?" Maria's right. I guess. I don't know about no extra points, though. I don't know how petition signatures get counted, period. But while Aaron was helping me focus on getting the easy signatures, I forgot that this whole thing is about us and all the other kids like us that go to Booker T. who won't have anything to do after school if the school board takes away funding for our clubs for good.

When I think about it, I know the real reason why I took Aaron's advice. It felt easier. When I imagine performing on a stage or talking to a bunch of people I don't know, I get so awkward. It always feels especially weird talking to kids like me, and my words get stuck. Grown-ups always think I'm cute, but it's kids who think my head is too big or that I'm too short or who make it so hard to speak up in the first place cuz all of them always got something to say. Looking through her list and around me, it looks almost like Maria, C.J., and Camille got most of the kids here. I hope that means I still don't have to be the one to get them to care.

I DON'T WANNA TALK TO THE PEOPLE MY AGE.
THEY MAKE ME FEEL NERVOUS, ALL SCARED AND
AFRAID.
I HATE HEARING STUFF LIKE "YO HEAD'S SO BIG!"

CUZ IT HURTS WHEN IT'S COMING FROM THESE
MEAN OL' KIDS.

BUT IT'S NOT JUST BOBBY, IT'S OTHER ONES,
TOO.

IT'S LIKE ALL KIDS ARE MEAN (*EXCEPT THE D.O.G. CREW*).
SO I'D RATHER JUST TALK TO GROWN--UPS AND
OLD FOLKS.
AT LEAST THAT WAY, I DON'T GOTTA HEAR JOKES!

AT LEAST THAT WAY, I CAN FEEL OKAY.
EVEN THOUGH *I KNOW* THEY PROLLY FEEL THE
SAME WAY.
AT LEAST THE ADULTS KEEP IT IN THEIR MINDS.
BUT THESE KIDS AIN'T KIND, SO THEY PROLLY
WON'T SIGN.
WOOF WOOF!

"Gosh, Maria, can't you just tell Simon the truth?" Camille shoves the back of Maria's head but she doesn't say anything. "Simon, these kids were already at this spot before we got over here.

Mami always gives out all the messed-up empanadas to kids who help clean up around the truck for free. Word spread fast today," she says, moving her arms around this mini-crowd like she's showing off a surprise.

Maria's eyes look like her pupils have rolled all the way to the back of her eye sockets to never come back again. Every time Camille hangs with us she has to bust Maria's positivity bubble. She's super smart and all the teachers at Booker T. still talk about her like a superstar, but outside of that, Camille's kind of dry and always seems like she's just waiting for anything that has to do with us to be over.

Auntie Julia knocks on the food truck counter twice and chucks an empanada in the air without any more warning. "Think fast, mijo!" And because I can never think fast enough, Aaron catches the shrimp empanada—my favorite—that was meant for me. I knew it was my favorite by the pink wrapper. In seconds it's gone as if he didn't just eat a whole pretzel by himself an hour ago. I'd be mad about this but Uncle Edwin comes out the side door and hands me two more after Auntie Julia sees. "Your big brother is greedy, right? If I were you I'd go find somewhere to hide around here so you can eat in peace!" she says, winking at me while she fills up a customer's drink.

Maria's pupils come back to the front of her face and she drops her head on my shoulder for a few seconds before sliding one of the empanadas out of my hand like she's tryna take it without me noticing or asking. Best Friends Code says she doesn't have to this time. And this food truck is one of the new perks of being Maria's best friend. We both peel back the shiny pink food wrappers and steam puffs out of the holes that are poked into the top of the flaky crust, making us look like we're talking outside in the winter. While I take the first bite I remember how

much I miss eating Auntie Julia's cooking. Yeah, sometimes we go over to Maria's house and Ms. Estelle hooks us up with all the Puerto Rican food we can eat, but there's still something super special about how her mom cooks. Now everybody in Creighton Park knows what's up, making all the time Maria's parents have to work kinda worth it.

I step back to really look at the big silver delivery truck that Auntie Julia and Uncle Edwin basically turned into a restaurant. Uncle Edwin leans out the front window, where they've got straws and napkins, and waves Maria over.

"Aye, you think you could get Aunt Julia to throw me and the homies a couple more of them empanadas, bro?" Now Aaron wants to be cool with me when less than an hour ago he tried to get rid of us. I look behind and Brandon and Rashad are back. Of course, he has to feed the minions. I ignore him until something pops into my head now that Maria's far enough away again for her not to hear.

"You think this is gonna work?" I ask him instead

of answering his question, and he ignores me back. "Why don't you ask Auntie Julia yourself?!"

"Because, *bro,* you the one that be goin' over they house. You family, *for real,* for real. She gon' make me pay just like Granny be makin' me pay for penny candy." Aaron has a point. Our own grandma, who's the neighborhood candy lady on her block, won't even let him sneak her cheapest candy for free. Something about the fact that he's in high school now means all the grown-ups we know make sure they give him an extra-hard time about how things work in the real world. They make everything a lesson about life and always say they're gettin' him ready to pay bills but it don't really work. Even though he got him a weekend job at Mr. Ray's shop and everything, he still rather use me to get what he wants so he can save his money for more important things. Like silk durags and Nike slides. Things Moms always says are for people with grown-people money.

"Fine. I'll ask Maria, but can you help me?"

"What was the question?"

"Do you think this petition thingy is gonna work?!"

"I'm not even gon' hold you, bro. The way you doin' it is extra boring. This what they *used* to do in the old days. We're *in* the *future* and y'all came out here with some notebooks." I know Aaron is for once tryna help but hearing his words makes me feel like the inflatable ball pit at the end of block parties after they let all the air out. "Just seems kind of old-school to me."

"But Mr. James said—"

"Listen to me. I know what these teachers be sayin' in class. All the stuff they teach in them ancient-history books. But things is different now. People ain't got time for all that. Ain't nobody finna be reading all that." When I asked for Aaron's help I didn't expect him to tell me all this might as well be for nothing. "Look, y'all tryna do something big for *real*?" He pauses to pull out his phone. "You need one of these." He unlocks the screen, opens up one of his apps, and starts moving the screen up with his thumb. I don't know what I'm supposed to be looking for but I already can't look away, seeing things like the *#ArtChallenge*, videos of kids hitting the Renegade on repeat, and some grown-ups eating chips in front of a microphone.

I THOUGHT THIS PETITION IDEA SOUNDED SWEET
BUT NOW AARON'S TELLIN' ME THIS STUFF IS
KINDA WEAK.
HE'S SAYIN' THAT IT'S OLD--SCHOOL AND NEEDS
A FEW TWEAKS
BUT HOW'S IT "OLD--SCHOOL" IF WE LEARNED IT
THIS WEEK?

WHAT WE 'SPOSE TO DO? LAY DOWN IN THE
STREET?
HOLD HANDS TOGETHER? ACT LIKE WE ASLEEP?
THAT WOULD NEVER HAPPEN CUZ MY MOMS
WOULD NEVER LET IT!

I CAN HEAR HER NOW, SAYING: "SIMON! FORGET
IT!"
GETTING SIGNATURES AIN'T THE GREATEST, I
ADMIT IT.
BUT AT LEAST IT'S *SOMETHIN'*, SO I'MA STICK WIT' IT.
GOTTA START SOMEWHERE IF WE WANNA MAKE
CHANGE

SO WE'LL KEEP WALKIN' ROUND TILL WE GET A
BUNCHA NAMES.

PLUS, MARIA WANTS THIS, SO I WANT IT, TOO!
I GOTTA HELP MY FRIEND FROM THE D.O.G.
CREW!
NAME AFTER NAME IS THE GOAL, THE MISSION,
UNTIL ALL OF CREIGHTON PARK SIGNS THE
PETITION!
WOOF WOOF!

"What you saying, Aaron? I gotta get a phone for people to pay attention to me?"

"Look, let's do it like this: You walk over there and get Aunt Julia to hook us up with like five more empanadas and I'll get on Twitter and tell errbody on the West Side about what my lil bro is doing." Aaron don't know everybody on the West Side. "Then I'ma get on Instagram and post a lil something about y'all's open mic tomorrow," he says, pointing to a post like the one he'll make for us. "Y'all doin' that again, right?" Part of me doesn't trust a word Aaron's saying. Most days he acts like he can't stand the fact that I even exist and now he wants to tell his friends about our little cause. The other part of me feels like this is what we been missing this whole time. I just didn't know how to say it.

"Yeah" is all I say. I don't know if I believe him all the way. Even though Aaron's good at this stuff.

"Got you, bro."

SUNDAY

CHAPTER 12

LAST TIME THE FAMILY WENT TO CHURCH was when the summer heat was hottest. Me, Aaron, DeShawn, and Markus were counting down the days till school opened back up so we could flex on everybody like we left as scrubs and came back new. Don't everybody do that? Everybody does that. It was like a month before the first day and Dad told us the night before that we better lay our clothes out. *I ain't about to let you sit up in them pews looking a mess so don't try nothin' funny like telling me you don't have nothin' to wear.* Even though it seems like church is chiller these days than what

Dad described when he was a kid, he still sort of makes us dress up on the Sundays that we go. That last time was important, Dad had said. Pastor Mike asked all the parents to make sure they brought their whole family so he could bless the kids before we went back to school. And by bless, he means he's gonna make sure all of us leave with a big oily cross on our foreheads. It didn't bother me much cuz I kinda like going, unlike my brothers. Since we don't go every Sunday, Dad always gives a speech the Saturday before so he don't have problems in the morning.

This Sunday, though, like most Sundays, Dad doesn't make a big deal about it cuz of my new weekly responsibility: Creighton Park Community Outreach Open Mics. Ever since I started hosting them on Sundays after the first one we had for Sunny, our parents don't really treat us like we're being lazy when we ask for twenty more minutes of sleep. They know we gotta get up and eventually head down the block to CPCO to set up. And by we, I mean me, Dad, DeShawn, and Markus. C.J. and Maria always meet us there and Moms takes as long as she feels like cuz she does a lot of the cooking the night before.

Today Miss Wanda comes huffing and puffing up the sidewalk to the front door of the shelter at the same time as us sorta looking like she went to a funeral even though we all know she came straight from church to open up. She's dressed in a black suit with white gloves and a matching white hat that looks like the ones they be wearing in Paris. Everybody knows the hats. The ones they always wearing in pictures. Hers has a piece of see-through cloth that goes over her eyes and stops right under her nose. We can hear the muffled sound of the organ, drums, and a few tambourines still going at Ebenezer Pentecostal Sanctuary coming from a short block away behind her. She puts bags she was carrying into our hands so she can unlock the front door.

A breeze floats the smell of cinnamon coming off Ms. Wanda's skin down to my nose, and I sneeze before I can stop myself. Peering down at me, she looks like all the old ladies who always got strawberry candies and mints in their purse. She gives me a look that makes me flash back to that last time we were at Ebenezer before school started and a white glove just like hers appeared under Aaron's mouth when he'd been caught chewing gum during service.

"I hope you not catching a cold, little man," she says, when we make eye contact. That white glove was Ms. Wanda's, and I can't believe I didn't recognize her the first time Dad introduced me last month. I shiver, glad it wasn't me who'd had to spit gum out in front of everybody. It's one of like a hundred reasons Aaron and Moms don't really like going but Grandma Lucille used to take Dad every week when he was a boy. So, sometimes, when the rest of the house rather sleep and Dad wants to go, he tells us we could at least go sometimes out of respect for his mama. But he never has to beg me.

I LIKE GOING TO CHURCH AND PRAISING THE
LORD.
IT'S NOT LIKE SCHOOL, SO YOU CAN'T GET
BORED.

ERRBODY IN THERE BE DOIN' THE MOST,

ESPECIALLY WHEN FOLKS CATCH THE HOLY
GHOST!

AND THAT PASTOR MIKE, HE SHO BE PREACHIN'.
THAT MASS CHOIR, THEY SHO BE SCREECHIN'.
BUT REALLY THEY SOUND GOOD, IT'S LOW--KEY
DECENT.

I BE WIDE AWAKE BUT MY BROS BE SLEEPIN'.
THE ORGAN'S PLAYIN', THE CHOIR'S SWAYIN'.
THE CHURCH MOTHERS UP IN THE FRONT BE
PRAYIN'.

IT ALL SOUNDS GOOD AND FEELS GOOD TO ME.
THE NOTORIOUS D.O.G. AND G--O--D!

At 2:45 p.m., almost exactly an hour later, Ms. Wanda goes back to the front door to prop it open, and people come flooding in as if they'd been waiting outside in a line. Moms is behind the shelter kitchen counter, passing large tin trays of hot food out to DeShawn and Markus so they can put it out onto the burners already set up along the food tables. For a minute I'm frozen in space seeing all the people walk in. We've pretty much had the same crowd every Sunday: people who are experiencing

homelessness and eat at the shelter all the time, my family, my squad, and a few teachers from Booker T. But this crowd is way younger. First, I see Aaron, who Dad never makes come to the shelter early to help set up, walk in with Brandon and Rashad. They check out the food table and find seats in the back to eat whatever they snuck when Moms wasn't looking. But then more high school kids start walking in. Some of them look like people I've seen hooping with Aaron on Locust but most of them are people I've never seen before. And there's way more than I ever expected. I watch them for a second, glad I made signs last night to put up around the shelter. We're using the open mic to get more signatures today and I couldn't imagine having to get our message across just using our actual voices. With all these people, a microphone just doesn't seem like enough.

Dad will never let C.J. help him do sound check—or come anywhere near the stage, really—after how annoying he was the first time, so I'm up on the stage we built together making sure everything is there and set up properly. Mic? Check.

Mic stand? Check. Loudspeakers? Check. Signs? I should probably go grab those now and start putting them up! I look across the room toward the food table and see that Moms got C.J. setting up all the cups, napkins, and plates but is still not letting him handle the really big trays of food. Baby steps. I hear Maria welcoming people in like she's already the mayor of Chi-town.

I step off the stage to get the signs out of my backpack, and I feel a deep pit form in my stomach at a thought. Our bedroom floor, covered in dirty drawers and sweaty socks, flashes before my eyes. Sticking out from under my bed, next to my backpack, is the stack of signs I stayed up last night making but didn't think to pack. I forgot the signs! Ugh. I hear Dad's voice boom from behind me. "Showtime in five minutes, big man!" I start to unzip my bag, feeling my heart pounding faster and faster against the inside of my chest as it crawls up my throat. Another flashback. This time: our bathroom sink. Covered in brushes, grease, toothpaste, and an empty toilet paper roll sit the flash cards with all my notes that I rehearsed all morning. I pat

my whole body with both my hands, knowing the flashback means one terrible thing: I forgot those, too. Face-palm emoji. *What am I going to say to all these people now?* I can't go up there unprepared!

Sweat starts to pool under my pits, all over my neck and forehead, and I just hope nobody is noticing me panic. I look across the sea of people starting to take their seats for the open mic and all their faces go blurry. My eyes search the whole room for Maria. She always knows what to do when things like this happen. She always knows what to say.

But that would ruin the whole point of the stuff I stayed up last night making, hoping somehow I could show my best friend that what happened to her club makes me sad, too. The last thing I wanna do is make it seem like she's the only one trying to fix things around here. *Come on, Simon, you've done this before. So many times. It's nothing.* Who am I kidding? I've never done it without a plan. Not without notes in my hands. Not on the fly. But could I...should I...

Maybe.

CHAPTER 13

IT SEEMS LIKE THE WHOLE CROWD LEANS back and cringes when I step up to the mic and a painful squeak from the loudspeakers pierces the air. A little shocked by it, I jump back and slide the mic stand a little farther away. If it wasn't for how long this day already feels I'd think I was dreaming, the way all these eyes are on me, everybody completely silent. Mr. James would call this being able to *hear a pin drop* but let's be real: Who's ever heard that? Today it might have been possible. Almost like the first open mic we had here, the room is full wall to wall and everybody in here is waiting on me to say something about why we're here but all I can think about is how I forgot my things at home. I look down at my hands, thinking, maybe, if I stared hard enough, I might be able to imagine the flash cards in my hands. Then, maybe, I could imagine what I wrote on them. But all I find in my palms is sweat and too many nerves that make me so shaky I force myself to wrap my hands tight around the mic stand so my hands have something to do. I look down, a few rows past C.J., to see Sunny nodding like he can hear his favorite song. He smiles and flicks his hand at me like he's waiting for me to finish saying whatever I have to say.

"G-g-good afternoon, everybody." Great, already stuttering. "W-we... w-w-we are here because...," I say, trying again. I look over at Maria at the side of the stage and she's smiling up at me. For a second my brain replays the day of our practice oral presentations in class on the first week of school when she had the exact same smile on her face. My belly starts to flip and get all woozy the same way it did that day as I remember the taste of spaghetti sauce coming up my throat while trying to push through

something I wasn't prepared for. And even then, I at least had flash cards. From outside, I hear a car's speakers as it drives by with music blasting and bass so deep that the wall closest to the street rattles like a tiny earthquake. I look over at C.J. in his seat, bobbing his head to a beat we've both heard before, and when the car passes he starts to clap the rhythm, and in seconds, so is everybody else.

WHEN I SAY "GIVE US," Y'ALL SAY "THE CLUBS!"
GIVE US (THE CLUBS!), GIVE US (THE CLUBS!)
WHEN I SAY "GIVE US," Y'ALL SAY "THE CLUBS!"
GIVE US (THE CLUBS!), GIVE US (THE CLUBS!)

MY BEST FRIEND MARIA IS SO SMART.
SHE TALKS A WHOLE LOT, BUT IT'S ALWAYS FROM
THE HEART.
AND SHE REALLY CARES FOR THE FOLKS IN
CREIGHTON PARK,
SO YOU PROLLY WON'T STOP HER FROM DEBATIN'
IF SHE STARTS!

JUST TAKE NOTES WHILE MARIA TAKES A STAND.
SHE HAS IT ALL MAPPED OUT, ALWAYS WITH A PLAN.

CHICAGO PUBLIC SCHOOLS TOOK AWAY THE
PROGRAMS,

BUT IF ANYONE CAN GET 'EM BACK, I KNOW
MARIA CAN!

DEBATE... KARATE... THEATER... AND ART,
ALL OF THOSE THINGS GOT CANCELED FROM
THE START.
WE NEED TO GET 'EM BACK SO KIDS CAN KEEP
A SPARK.
BOOKER T. NEEDS CLUBS LIKE A DOG NEEDS A
BARK.

SO WHEN I SAY "GIVE US," Y'ALL SAY "THE
CLUBS!"
GIVE US (THE CLUBS!), GIVE US (THE CLUBS!)
WHEN I SAY "GIVE US," Y'ALL SAY "THE CLUBS!"
GIVE US (THE CLUBS!), GIVE US (THE CLUBS!)

UP NORTH, THEY GOT IT GOOD, THAT'S TRUE.
BUT SCHOOLS OUT WEST NEED PROGRAMS, TOO!
IT'S NOT REALLY FAIR IF THE KIDS UP THERE
ARE THE ONLY ONES WITH MONEY AND SUPPLIES
TO SHARE.

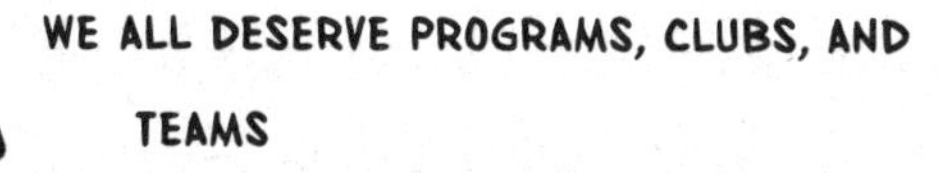

WE ALL DESERVE PROGRAMS, CLUBS, AND
TEAMS

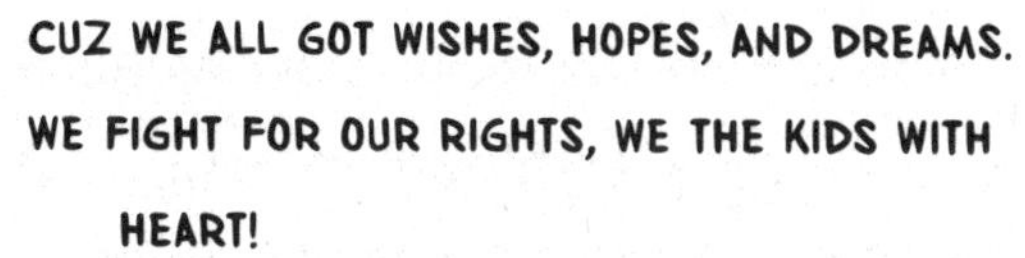

CUZ WE ALL GOT WISHES, HOPES, AND DREAMS.
WE FIGHT FOR OUR RIGHTS, WE THE KIDS WITH
HEART!
WE JUST ASK THAT YOU JOIN US AND PLAY YOUR
PART!

SO WHEN I SAY "GIVE US," Y'ALL SAY "THE
CLUBS!"
GIVE US (THE CLUBS!), GIVE US (THE CLUBS!)
WHEN I SAY "GIVE US," Y'ALL SAY "THE CLUBS!"
GIVE US (THE CLUBS!), GIVE US (THE CLUBS!)

"AAAAAAYYYY!" Out the corner of my eye I see Aaron run up the aisle like one of those people who fall out at the altar in church. But he don't fall out when he gets to the stage. He hops up and shakes my hand, still recording me while the rest of the room cheers loudly from their seats. Even though I'm done rapping, C.J.'s at the edge of the stage making drumroll sounds with his hands on the floor. Aaron turns the camera to himself, slinging his arm around my neck as I start walking off the stage. I've never seen Aaron this happy about anything I did. Maria takes the mic and squeezes my hand on her way up to the stage as Aaron pulls me into view on his phone's camera. "MY BRO GOT BARS! MY BRO GOT BARS, BOY! WHO'S NEXT?! WHO WANT SOME?!"

Down the steps, and as I walk down the aisle Aaron just ran from, hands reach out to me to dap me up, squeeze my shoulders, pat my back, and give me high fives that pull into hugs. One of those hugs comes from C.J., who follows me with our notebooks after I finally get offstage to get ready to collect signatures. It's kind of hard to believe all these people are showing me love after doing one of the scariest things, but at the same time it sort of feels right. Dad pulls both me and C.J. into his stomach and turns us to face the stage, putting his arms around both our shoulders. Ms. Wanda hushes the crowd to make sure we all listen to Maria. Dad slips the notebooks out of our hands and pulls us closer in.

"Why don't you two go on back up near the front so y'all can watch and support your friend," sounding more like he's telling us than asking.

"But Uncle David, we have to—"

"Now, now, now. Don't you worry about it, Cornelius. I got it covered, okay? Maria needs your support. She needs to see y'all up there. Go on," Dad says, nudging our backs toward the front. We listen to him but I can't help but look back behind me and see Dad whispering to DeShawn and Markus.

I don't know about C.J. but I'm glad Dad made us go back to our seats. Sitting in the front row watching one of my best friends do her thing brings all the reasons we're here back to my mind. I don't know that many other fifth graders can stand onstage looking the way she does right now. She's probably a little scared cuz Moms always tells us it happens to everybody. But what's even wilder is that she doesn't just look confident, she looks like she really likes being up there. She's talking to a room full of mostly strangers like a G. No flash cards or heebie-jeebies in sight.

Next to the stage, Aaron kneels down where Maria can't see and takes out his phone again, holding it up enough to get her on camera without noticing. He's so tall it always looks funny when he squats down to our size. I see him hold down the record button and his mouth hangs open the whole time, moving into different awkward positions to get the best shots. I didn't know he'd done the same for me until I was finished, and I bet it's best that Maria doesn't know he's recording, either. She looks so calm and serious but cameras always change things.

"...We are growing kids who need things to do after school to help us keep learning. And clubs aren't just something to do. They help us focus and make us creative so when we grow up we know how to finish things and solve big problems in the future. Please sign our petition telling the school board Booker T. needs our money back. Thank you!" Everybody stands up to cheer for her and when she walks down the stairs to sit next to me and C.J., I'm clapping so hard the insides of my hands sting and turn red but I can't help it. The only thing that would have made her ending more perfect is if she'd dropped the mic, but I can already hear Moms in my ear. *Does she have mic-dropping money?* Sure don't.

Ms. Wanda trades spots with Maria and we hear her repeat some of the things Maria said while she was onstage. It sounds a lot less cool when she does it. Ms. Wanda doesn't at all sound like she's got the juice like Ri-Ri. She moves on with the scheduled program, letting everybody know there's a sign-up for the open mic near the stage so they don't get it confused with the petition. Wait. The petition!

Right then, while everybody is told to take a ten-minute break, Dad taps me on the shoulder and tells us to follow him to the back, where DeShawn and Markus are sitting with our notebooks.

"Why do they—" Maria starts, and Dad holds up a hand.

"Hold on, baby girl, they were here to help. While you were up there talking your talk, these two got y'all started." For a minute I wonder how much Dad promised them for this.

"Yo, you kilt it up there, bro," Markus says.

"And Ri-Riiiii, I ain't know you had the Michelle Obama–level skills. Okay, okay!" Maria blushes under DeShawn's compliments. Before this, both of them pretty much spoke to her like they do me. To tell her to move, be quiet, or mind her business. Not this time, though. They're even sort of treating both of us like celebrities. Feels kinda good but still weird.

"So here you go. You got a good jump start. Now all you gotta do is get the rest." They hand both of the notebooks to us and point out the people who signed already and the people who didn't. This time we agree that Maria will get kids' signatures and I'll hit up the grown-ups on purpose. C.J. will stick with me. Since a lot of people are using the break to get food, C.J. comes up with the idea to set up near the beginning of the food table so people can sign their names before making their plates. Genius. And they already know what for? Let's go!

The last open-mic performer gets onstage just as me, Maria, and C.J. sit down, exhausted from talking to so many people. Moms comes out of the kitchen and puts three steaming plates in front of us, and for just a second it feels like we're in Grandma Lucille's dining room on Thanksgiving sitting at the kids' table with grown-up-sized plates. All three plates look like we went back for seconds and thirds while still on the first plate, and none of us are mad about it. Aaron reaches toward my plate for a deviled egg, and Moms swats his hand away like a fly.

"These plates are for the *activists*," she tells him, winking at me.

"But Ma! What about the cameraman?"

"Where was the cameraman when the activists were *working* the room just now?" Moms asks. Aaron drops his head and scratches the back of his neck as if to say *Aight, you got me,* then grabs a biscuit, stuffing the whole thing in his mouth. Moms is too shocked to even get mad. And I wasn't gonna eat it anyway. "Boy, you a whole mess. Acting like you didn't start eating the second you and your little friends walked in here. Yeah, I saw you. Got a stomach like a bottomless pit."

I picture watching everything Aaron eats come out the other end like none of it was even chewed and I start laughing so hard grape pop squirts out my nose and drizzles on top of my candied yams. "Bet he won't try to steal nothin' from that plate now," Moms says, looking disgusted. Aaron finally swallows the last big chunk of my biscuit and clears his throat.

"But nah, for real, bro. We gotta put this up on Instagram. When other kids see this online they gon' go brazy! You had bars on bars on bars," Aaron tells me, pacing around the table. None of us have any room in our mouths to say anything so he goes on. "And Ri-Riiiii. Sis. You too." He pauses and looks over at our parents. They're the ones who really get to say if Aaron's footage can get posted or not. Ms. Wanda starts to close out the open mic, and two hands come reaching from behind Maria and wrap her in a hug. Before I see her, I know it's Auntie Julia. When her and Uncle Edwin aren't fresh off work she always smells like lemons. Maria turns around and almost leaps into her arms.

"Mamiiiiiii!" None of us knew they were coming.

"You did so *good*, mija! Look at you. My little

activista." Maria is crying. It's a serious moment and all that, but all I can focus on is how different Maria's parents look out of their work uniforms. Usually, they're both wearing matching red T-shirts with the same logo that's on the side of their food truck: a cartoon version of an empanada that has a face, floating down a lake with the city skyline behind it. Usually, Auntie Julia has her big curly hair stuffed under a hairnet, and Uncle Edwin's hand tattoos are covered by gloves. Uncle Edwin wipes Maria's tears with his thumbs and kisses her on her forehead just as Mr. James stops by on his way out.

"Aww, yeah, there they go!" He pauses to greet all the adults while keeping his eyes on us. "That was amazing, y'all. Real powerful stuff. We might have a young community organizer in the making, y'all. That was real leadership right there." He daps all three of us up before shaking Aaron's hand, pulling him into a hug. "Good to see you, man. You mind sending me that video?"

"I got you, Mr. James," Aaron agrees.

"Y'all have a good night."

"So as I was saying... I got videos of both y'all that I'm tryna put on my Instagram and TikTok. Can I?" This question is for all the grown-ups. Back when Aaron got his first cell phone Dad gave him a whole speech about asking permission before he posts pictures or videos of other people on his social media. He called it consent and said he better not ever see any pics or videos of me, DeShawn, or Markus floating around online without asking him and Moms first or Aaron's social life is over. Me and Maria look up at our parents and wait.

"*Only* if you put some respect on my baby's name. It's Maria to y'all and *Miss* Maria Rivera, the activista, to the world!" Maria blushes even harder than she did when Mr. James called her a leader.

"So... is that a yes?"

Moms, Dad, and Maria's parents look at each other and nod, and Dad answers for the whole group:

"You have our consent. Go for it."

CHAPTER 14

TONIGHT AFTER THE OPEN MIC, EVERY-body seems too tired to care about anything else, so Moms and Dad let everybody do their own thing for dinner. Moms tells us we can eat whatever we want as long as it's in the house and we don't ask them to do any type of cooking. After announcing this, her and Dad leave us in the kitchen to figure things out for ourselves. Aaron pulls a mostly empty pizza box out of the fridge and takes it into his room. DeShawn and Markus raid the cabinets for all the last packs of ramen we have to make what they call Monster Ramen, where they put a whole bunch of flavors together and add random things from the fridge to upgrade it. But I've seen one of their Monster Ramens before: It's not an upgrade, friends. Not an upgrade at all. I gag just thinking about it, knowing I need to get out of the kitchen before it all goes down.

So I pull a stool up to the counter next to the fridge, climb up, and pull out my stash of Fruity-O's from the cabinets above the fridge in the back of some baking stuff that never gets used. I pour it into a huge silver bowl. I pull out some milk I hid behind a big pot in the fridge and take it all to the couch, where Markus already turned on the TV. The kitchen starts smelling funny about five minutes later and I realize I gotta eat as fast as I can and get out of here.

In the bathroom I brush my teeth over our sink that's still covered in all the stuff we left out in our rush to get to the shelter this morning. When I bend down to spit out a mouth full of toothpaste water, my eyes can't help but go straight to the flash cards full of all the things I scribbled trying to make sure I knew exactly what to say onstage. *The school took away my best friend's after-school club last week. She'd been excited about it all summer. We need your help telling CPS that it isn't fair. We deserve these programs on the West Side, too.* I put my mouth under the running faucet and rinse. I look back into the mirror and can't help but smile imagining everybody in the room watching me freestyle with nothing in my hands. Somehow I still knew what I wanted to say even though I'd left the things I thought I needed at home.

"Looks like Simon let the Notorious D.O.G. out the house tonight," Moms says just after she knocks on the already-open door. She folds her arms and leans into the door behind me. Her hair is pulled back into her silk bonnet and she's wearing a big purple nightshirt that looks like she could fit five Moms in it. She caught me smiling at myself in the mirror and all of a sudden I feel a little weird. "How you feelin'?"

I feel my face get all hot under this question, and I don't really know what to say. So much happened

so fast, and it definitely could have gone a whole different way. The truth is I messed up so many times, forgetting all the stuff I made for our open mic today, and things could have really been bad. What if I can't magically freestyle the next time I forget my notes? What if leaving all my stuff at home could have cost us a whole bunch of support? What if everything we did doesn't really matter and tomorrow we go back to a school that has no plans to give my best friend her club back?

"It's okay if you don't have the words right now, baby," Moms says, pulling me to her and kissing the top of my head. "Today was a lot, and it makes sense if you don't know how you feel about it. I just want you to know me and your daddy are so proud of you and how you showed up for your friend today. You might not know it but what you did was big. Maria is lucky to have a friend like you." Before Moms leaves me smiling at myself in the bathroom she points to my flash cards with her chin. "Didn't need those after all, huh?"

My mind replays all the high school kids' faces looking up at me onstage. Aaron said I got *bars* and was recording me. Everything went so good that I almost can't believe it. For a few minutes I'm not in the bathroom that I share with my brothers. I close my eyes and I'm back onstage in front of a bunch of people waiting to hear whatever it was we had to say. Today couldn't have been more perfect even if it had gone exactly as planned.

"Aye, Smiley Face, your little happy self needs to go on somewhere. I gotta whiz." Aaron lightly jabs my stomach and puts me in a soft headlock before letting me leave. I trash the flash cards on the sink, turn the light out, and close the door right before he starts to pee. A few steps down the hall, Aaron lets me know through the door that he's gonna get me back. But for now, I win the bathroom light wars. The soft headlock lets me know I'll get a pass.

Aye, Smiley Face, he said. Without saying that much, even Aaron noticed how today made me feel. Today was good for everybody.

MONDAY

CHAPTER 15

5:57 A.M. WHEN MY EYES OPEN, I CAN tell it's still dark outside by the super-dark greenish-blue color of our room. It doesn't get that much light even when the sun is out because of all the stuff DeShawn and Markus have piled up against the walls next to their beds. Usually there's just enough light coming in to let me know it's morning, though. I clutch my chest, feeling yanked out of my sleep by a vision that I thought was only happening to the dream version of me. I feel goose bumps pop up all over me and pull the covers back over my head to go back asleep. *Nope. Nope. Nope. Not* *today, Simon. Not today.* I turn over to my stomach and squeeze my eyes back shut, replaying yesterday, hoping I doze off into a happier dream. A dream where I don't mess anything up and I'm celebrating with my homies. As my eyelids get heavy, I see our parents surrounding me, Maria, and C.J. while we inhale the heaps of food Moms brought out especially made for us. I see myself sitting next to my two best friends feeling happy but tired after all the talking and questions, making sure we asked everybody for help. It all went so fast I don't even remember holding the notebook after all that. *Guard this with your life.... We can't mess...*

7:04 a.m. Moms' fist against the door yanks me out of my sleep, and when I see the time glowing from Markus's alarm clock across the room, I know she let us sleep in. Four extra minutes is big for Moms on a Monday. When I'm out of the bathroom and dressed, I walk into the kitchen to see a stack of pancakes on the kitchen counter waiting for me next to Dad, and I shrug off the bad dream

I woke up from earlier. Yesterday was perfect and Dad made breakfast, so it's a perfect morning, too.

"Rise and shine." Dad clears his newspapers off the counter to make space for me and goes to turn on the TV while I sit down. "How you feeling, man?"

"Hungry," I tell him. It's the truth. Cereal for dinner is good and all, but my stomach feels way too empty, like everything I ate yesterday went right through me. Maybe this explains the way Aaron eats before and after his games. I fold a pancake in half like a taco and stuff a huge chunk of it into my mouth.

"Sounds about right," Dad says from behind me, keeping it extra short. One of my favorite parts about Dad making breakfast is how he knows when I want to talk and when we don't need to. Plus, he knows I've been eating pancakes like this since I was like five and there's no point in tryna rap me up with a mouth full of pancake. Besides, even though I'm way bigger than I was when I started eating them like this, everybody still gets scared that I might choke, so they've stopped distracting me while I eat. They need to relax, though. I'm eleven, a whole professional.

Dad flips the channel with his newspaper spread across the coffee table while I continue stuffing my face and watching the clock for when Maria and Ms. Estelle will be getting here. "Thanks, Dad," I say as he comes back into the kitchen to sit back at the counter. I rinse my plate and put it in the sink.

"A whole lotta people came out yesterday, huh?"

"I've never seen that many people at the shelter before!"

"Had to be at least a hundred people up in there, for sure," he says.

"For real?!"

"Oh yeah, for sure. You count all them signatures yet? That'll tell you."

The feeling I woke up with, thinking it was a dream, comes back strong, and all of a sudden I'm extra woozy like the room just got done spinning. Trying not to look as freaked out by the small thought that won't go away, I speed-walk back to my room. Once past Dad's view I run to the side of my bed, where I tossed my backpack last night. I fall onto my knees and yank it open, pushing things aside, then dumping everything on the floor when that starts to take too long. A notebook falls out onto the floor and I almost cry when I flip it over and see the cover marked MATH. I look back into my empty backpack and turn it over, shaking it as hard as I can. This can't be right. It's not right. Nope, nope, nope. I'm just looking in the wrong place is all.

"What are you *doing*?" Markus asks in the way people ask if they think you look stupid. I look up

for a second, then keep searching. DeShawn walks out of the room and I hear him laughing all the way to the bathroom. I'm definitely looking in the wrong place. I probably left it on the couch when we got home, yes! *It's in the living room, duh. That's probably why Dad asked me if I counted yet because he probably counted. Exactly.*

Dad appears in the doorway. "Did you hear me, son? Did you count 'em yet? Or are y'all waiting to do that after school today? I'm ready to see the numbers!" He's rubbing his hands together, smiling like he knows he has a winning lottery ticket and he's just waiting for it to be announced on TV.

7:40 a.m. I swear this is the cleanest I've ever seen the living room, the couch, the coffee table, and the kitchen counter be in my whole life. Not even Dad's newspaper is left out. And it's so hot in here. *Why is it so freaking HOT?! It's supposed to be fall!* I start to pull at my T-shirt collar to get some air but no amount of fanning does anything. I feel sweat starting to drip down my neck to my stomach and am moving too quick around the living room, lifting couch cushions, remote controls, and shoes to notice Dad has followed me back out of my room and has been watching me from the kitchen counter this whole time. I think the room really is spinning this time and sit down before I end up putting Saturday's chin dive on repeat.

OKAY, SIMON--FOCUS, FOCUS.
USE A LITTLE MAGIC, HOCUS--POCUS!
THINK FOR A SECOND...OKAY, GO LOOK!
ABRACADABRA! WHERE IS THAT NOTEBOOK?!
IT MUST BE IN THE FREEZER, OR WAS IT IN THE
    STOVE?

THE DRESSER? THE SHOWER? IT'S PROLLY ONE
    OF THOSE!
HOLD UP A SECOND, I KNOW WHERE I LEFT IT!
ON TOP OF THE ROOF! THAT'S RIGHT, I GUESSED IT!
I THINK...I HOPE...I BEG...I PRAY!
YOU *DIDN'T* LOSE THE NOTEBOOK, SI, THERE'S
    NO WAY!

THE D.O.G. WOULD NEVER DO A THING LIKE THAT
AND MESS UP MARIA'S PLANS TO GET THE
    MONEY BACK.

NEVER!

RIGHT?

WRONG!

WOOF!

"What's goin' on, Si?" I hear Dad say. He comes into focus through my fists that I'm now using to rub my eyes. When this doesn't stop the room from spinning, I close my eyes and give up. Tears start falling down the sides of face, into my ears, and down my neck. I can't get myself to answer him. I can't get myself to tell Dad that I can't find the notebook with all my signatures in it. The one Maria warned me to guard with my life that I ended up losing anyway. I can't say any of those words to him cuz it would mean I *really* ruined things and kids at Booker T. won't have a chance at getting our clubs back because of me.

"We have to find it, Dad. We just have to or Maria's going to hate me!"

"Whoa, whoa, whoa, slow down, son. That's one of your best friends. She could never do anything like that."

"But I messed everything up!"

Dad doesn't ask any more questions after I say that. He takes out his cell phone, dials a number, and walks into the kitchen. The doorbell rings. The clock on the wall says it's 7:51. *Maybe if I just sit here quietly they'll go away. Maybe Dad saw it and he's just waiting for me to calm down before he gives it back to me. Maybe if I wish hard enough it'll stop being Monday morning altogether.* I squeeze my eyes shut as hard as I can and open them back up as Dad walks back into the living room and sits down on the couch. Feels like the same day to me. The doorbell rings. And Maria and Ms. Estelle are outside.

I use the bottom of my shirt to dry my face while Dad tells me he called the shelter. That Ms. Wanda looked around the shelter dining hall for the notebook but it's nowhere to be found.

CHAPTER 16

WE PASS THE LOCUST BASKETBALL COURT before I even look at Maria. I listen to her go on and on about how excited she is to show Ms. Berry what we've done until we turn into the Booker T. parking lot. I don't want to tell my best friend that I've disappointed her. That I lost half of the signatures we got, being stupid and clumsy. She never should have trusted me with something so big. I always get scared and forget things when I get put on the spot. Ms. Estelle drops us off at the bottom of the stairs and wishes us both luck. Buena suerte, mis amores. Before Maria can walk up the stairs, I jump in front of her and spit it out.

"Don't hate me."

"Oh em gee, Simon, why would I ever hate you?! You're my best fri—"

"I lost the notebook with my half of the signatures and I'm so sorry I looked for it everywhere and I can't find it and if you hate me now I understand I'm so so so sorry please forgive me," I say all at once before taking a breath.

At first, she just stands there looking at me. I wouldn't even know what kind of face to call the one she has right now.

"Did you hear what I said?"

"Oh. Uh, I mean, that's okay," she says before turning back around and walking into the school. Walking into Mr. James's class, I see Maria talking to C.J. in front of Mrs. Leary's across the hall. He looks back over at me and shakes his head but forces a fake smile. I know when C.J.'s smiles are fake.

Class feels weird without Maria turning around every few minutes to make faces at me or mess with me when Mr. James isn't looking. The way she said it was okay sounded more like she was saying *I'm so mad I'm just gonna be quiet.* I'd know. I've seen it on Moms a few times, dealing with the super-long list of things me and my brothers have done to our apartment by accident. It never goes on for that long but it never feels good to know you messed up.

About halfway through fifth period, when I don't think I can take another minute of Maria being mad at me, Mr. James's class phone rings. A few seconds after he picks it up, he's looking directly at both me and Maria. He hangs up and calls us both to his desk, telling us to pack up our stuff and go to the office. Ms. Berry wants to see us. The class hears him say this and an *ooooOOOoooo* goes through the room while kids watch us grab our things. We clean off our desks, grab our bags, and walk down the hall to Ms. Berry's office in silence.

STEP BY STEP...IT'S WAY TOO QUIET.
MARIA SAYS SHE'S OKAY...I DON'T BUY IT.
I COULD MAKE A JOKE...NOPE...I WON'T TRY IT.
ME AND THE WORLD'S BEST DEBATER KEEP
SILENT.

WE IN THIS HALLWAY AND I FEEL WAY SMALL
CUZ I CAN'T TALK TO MY BEST FRIEND AT ALL.
I'M THE ONE TO BLAME, IT'S ALL MY FAULT,
SO WE DON'T SAY A THANG IN THIS HALL...WE
WALK.

OUR GYM SHOES SQUEAK ON THIS DIRTY FLOOR.
KIDS TALKIN' REAL LOUD, TEACHERS CLOSIN'
DOORS.

EVEN WHEN SOMEBODY SAYS, "DON'T EAT THAT
GLUE!"
WE CAN'T LAUGH OUR HEADS OFF LIKE WE
WANTED TO.

IT'S JUST SILENCE....

Walking into Ms. Berry's office, I realize I've never actually been in here. At least not in a long time. Most of the walls are covered with pictures of her posing with kids and the rest of the office is stacks and stacks of books, folders, and binders. On her desk is just more books and pictures of her with kids, except the pictures on her desk look like they're with kids that are hers. I don't know why Ms. Berry would need all these books here when whenever I see her, she's walking through the halls, in a meeting, or watching us at recess or in the cafeteria. How could she ever have time to read?

We sit in two seats across from her, and she puts one of the biggest books she has at the corner of her desk in front of us. Then she pulls out her phone, scrolls a few times, and then flips it around so we can see the screen. She props it up on the big book and reaches around to press Play. On the screen, me and Maria watch yesterday's open mic at the shelter. But this time it's from the view of the audience, and I almost can't believe what I'm seeing. Notorious D.O.G. is *RIPPING* the stage. Wow! I sneak a look over at Maria and she's smiling just as hard as me. This is my first time ever hearing myself rhyme in front of an audience. The first time I'm getting to see people cheer for me while I'm doing my thing.

Maria puts her hand on my shoulder while we watch the crowd going wild for me. "Go, best friend. That's my best friend," she says, cheesing extra hard at the screen. Still best friends.

The video cuts from Aaron to Maria, and when I look over at her, she's cheesing even harder. When

the video's over she grabs my hand and I feel a light squeeze. *Maybe I didn't ruin everything after all.* We sit there holding hands for a second, smiling, and then I remember we still don't know why Ms. Berry called us in here. And how did Ms. Berry even get this? Is Ms. Berry on... Instagram?!

"Mr. James sent this to me last night, and I have to say... I'm pretty impressed." Me and Maria can't help but high-five. "You all created a lot of buzz around here. Great stuff. And... your friend Cornelius?"

Me and Maria look at each other.

"C.J.?" we both say.

"C.J.," Ms. Berry repeats, smiling a little bit. "He got to school early today to show me *this*." She slides a piece of paper closer to us so we can read. Luckily Ms. Berry explains, since our eyes aren't moving fast enough. "Your friend told me he had an assignment to write about someone he admires because of the changes they're making. And he wanted me to see the two-paragraph essay he wrote about *you*, Maria. I'm so impressed."

Maria is smiling so hard it kinda looks like her face hurts... in a good way. "SO WE COULD GET

ALL OUR CLUBS BACK?!" Maria asks, almost jumping out of her seat.

"Well, I heard there was a petition going around. Which is amazing, b—"

"Ooh, Ms. Berry, let me show you!" Maria says, cutting her off. And she turns around and pulls out the notebook that didn't get lost, handing it over to Ms. Berry. "There was *really* two times as many as this, but we had a few, um, technical difficulties," she says, squeezing my arm. Even after I've disappointed her, she still looks out for me.

Ms. Berry looks through Maria's pages and pages of names and chuckles to herself, tapping on the cover after she closes it. "I can't promise you anything just yet, but I'll see what I can do. I'm really proud of you both and what you've accomplished here all by yourselves. You should really give yourselves a pat on the back," Ms. Berry tells us, setting the notebook to the side and tapping it one last time. All of us are quiet for a few seconds while Maria looks around Ms. Berry's office like she's in a museum. "All right, let me walk you kids down to the cafeteria. The bell's gonna ring in about five minutes and today you've got time to get down there for first dibs before everybody else gets out of class. How does that sound?"

FIRST DIBS AT LUNCH SOUNDS DOPE, THAT'S A
FACT!

BUT I WANNA KNOW WILL WE GET OUR CLUBS
BACK?

WILL ALL OF THE SPEECHES, PETITIONS, AND
RAPS
DO ANYTHING GOOD TO PUT OUR CAUSE ON THE
MAP?

MS. BERRY TALKIN' 'BOUT "I'LL SEE WHAT I CAN DO.
YOU MADE A LOT OF BUZZ, AND I'M REALLY
PROUD OF YOU."
BUT WILL IT BE ENOUGH OR IS SHE JUST SAYING
STUFF?

I WONDER...I ALSO WONDER WHAT WE HAVE FOR
LUNCH.
OH YEAH...PIZZA PUFFS!

"Good," we both say at the same time. On our way out of Ms. Berry's office Maria stops by the door to stare at a picture of a girl with a huge Afro surrounded by a bunch of people who look like they're her friends. All of them look like they're screaming about something that made them angry even though they sort of still look like they're having fun. They all got signs in their hands that look like they made them themselves. Maria asks who the girl is.

Ms. Berry winks at us before leading us down the hallway out of her office: "Me."

ONE WEEK LATER

CHAPTER 17

"GOOD AFTERNOON, EVERYBODY. WEL-come to today's debate. My name is Jerrell Wright and I will be your chairperson. Next to me is Kenneth Brown, who will be my timekeeper. Mr. James will be our a-a-adj-adjudicator. The topic for today's debate: Chicago Public Schools should not take away funding for after-school programs at Booker T. The affirmative team will be led by Maria Rivera and the negative will be led by Stephanie Lee. The speaker for each side will have three minutes only. There will be a single bell at the halftime mark and a double bell when you have thirty seconds left.

When the final bell rings, the speaker must stop talking and go back to their seat. Now, I would like to i-i-introduce the first speaker on the affirmative team. Maria Rivera."

Maria walks into the middle of our classroom in between all the desks that were pushed to each side for both teams. Unlike me, she isn't shaking or sweating. She don't even look a little bit nervous. Today she has her baby-blue frames on that match the stripes in her shirt that match the patches in her pants that match the shoelaces in her Vans. I see her take the biggest breath the same way she does before she does anything that she's really excited about. Ms. Berry walks into the class and leans against the wall next to where Uncle Edwin and Auntie Julia are sitting. They flash their thumbs up when the principal looks their way.

Maria looks over at me and sticks her tongue out. I flex my bicep, and we both laugh at the inside joke nobody else but C.J. would get. I start thinking about everything that went down over the past few weeks. Nothing is really that different yet at Booker T. A bunch of kids that stay after school till their parents get off work still make it hard for kids to focus on anything but protecting themselves from flying dodgeballs and backpacks flung onto tables without looking. And a lot of times that's still where Mr. James has to take the kids in debate to practice. Who knows what's gonna happen next? All I know is the next time something's happening around us that don't seem fair, we got ways to tell people it's not okay and that somebody needs to do something about it. And there are people listening to us.

"My name is Maria Rivera, and today I'm going to be talking to you about why CPS should not take away our funding for after-school clubs at Booker T.," she says before pausing to make sure her flash cards are in the right order. She looks back at me and puts them in her pocket. Then Maria turns to Ms. Berry. "My name is Maria Rivera, and today I'm going to talk to you about why you shouldn't let CPS take away our clubs' funding.

"Firstly, art is in everything. People painted the walls. People wrote the books in our library. Somebody came up with the ideas for this building. This

Debate!

school wouldn't even be here if it wasn't for creativity. If you let CPS take Art Club from us, maybe one day they'll even think this school shouldn't be here, either.

"Secondly, there are people who studied music who found out music helps us kids focus. If Mr. James didn't make up cool songs for the things that are hard to remember, a lot of us wouldn't learn anything. Math would be boring without fun songs.

"Thirdly, all us kids learn all kinds of different ways. If you take away Karate Club, you make it harder for kids who like to move their body and their mind, which just isn't right." Auntie Julia and Uncle Edwin jump out of their seats, clapping and crying so hard it looks like they might break their own hands. "Mami, I'm not finished," Maria whispers across the room, even though all of us can hear.

"Sorry, sorry, go 'head, baby!"

"Ms. Berry, last week you told me and Simon that you would see what you could do. We worked really hard to show you that it isn't okay what's happening to us at our school. My cousin goes to a school on the North Side that has everything. They never take any of this stuff away from them, but people act like it doesn't matter over here," Maria says, pausing to take another breath.

"I guess what I'm trying to say is...is..." She looks back at me again. *What is it, Ri-Ri?*

"What I'm trying to say is...is...if you let the school board take away everything that so many of my friends were waiting all summer for, you would be telling us that we don't deserve these cool opportunities. And you don't believe *that,* do you, Ms. Berry?"

The Notorious D.O.G. don't know a whole lot about debate matches but it seems like Maria went off the script. By the look on Ms. Berry's face, I can tell Maria did something she wasn't supposed to do...or at least it wasn't something Ms. Berry expected.

Nobody moves in the room for what seems like forever, then Uncle Edwin clears his throat to shout, *"THAT'S MY BABY GIRL"* before running out into the middle of the room to scoop Maria up. Auntie Julia bursts into tears and now I'm *really* confused because I don't feel like there's anything to be sad about. It's actually one of the coolest things I've ever seen! Something I might feel too nervous to ever do. Now the whole room is standing and clapping for Maria while she walks back toward me to sit down.

"Yo! You SNAPPED, Ri-Ri!" C.J. can't help but say this before she even sits all the way down. "It was like... it was like you just blacked ALL THE WAY out! I don't know what y'all about to do next but I think you won the whole debate!"

"That's not even how debates work, silly," she says back to him, trying to sound all serious but sort of blushing at his comment. The whole room seems like it's moving after Maria's back in her seat, and looking around, it seems like everybody forgot what we came to do: watch a practice match in Mr. James's classroom. While Mr. James tries to get everybody to calm down, I see Ms. Berry use her pointer finger to call Maria over to her. Uh-oh. Nothing good could ever come from being called over by the principal in the middle of class. I mean, it *is* technically *after* school and I don't think you can get called to the office after school. And sure, we got called to Ms. Berry's office last week and nothing happened but that's the point, I guess. Nothing happened.

Maria squeezes my hand before she gets up to walk behind all the desks that are pushed close to the wall where Ms. Berry's standing. The class really gets quiet when Ms. Berry leans down and whispers something to her before they both walk out into the hallway. So far, still doesn't look too good for my friend but I don't know why she'd be in trouble, for real. She told the truth. And I've never seen a debate match before, but what just happened sounded legit except for the talking to Ms. Berry thing. Something tells me Maria was supposed to stick to her flash cards. She was supposed to stick to the plan. Somebody else on the other team is supposed be in the middle of the room arguing against what Maria said right now. But what could anybody say to disagree with her? She's right.

Maria walks back in the room right as Mr. James tries to start off the debate again, and everybody turns to watch her go back to her seat. She smiles all the way until she plops back down next to me.

"Ahem." Mr. James clears his throat to get everybody to turn back around, and I lean closer to Maria as soon as they all stop staring. I have to know what went down.

"SIMON!" Maria whisper-screams. "You see that lady over there next to Ms. Berry?" Maria picks the *worst* times to gossip.

"Um, no, can't say I can. But Maria, wha—"

"THAT'S THE SUPERINTENDENT OF CPS!" She pauses, waiting for me to react, but I don't know what Super Nintendo has to do with anything. The person she's pointing at just looks way too dressed up to be on the West Side. "She's, like, Ms. Berry's *BOSS*! She's one of those board people who could help us get our money back for all the clubs!" Maria's still sort of whisper-screaming but I can tell some other kids aren't minding their business by the way they're looking back at us.

"She said that? What happened?" I whisper back. At this point Mr. James gotta be pretending he can't hear us. Neither of us are good at the whisper-scream.

"I mean she said, *That was a very passionate speech you gave in there, Ms. Rivera.* Then she said, *We'll have to see what we can do to make sure the kids at Booker T. get the things you all need...* Isn't that great, Simon?! I can't believe it!" She doesn't even try to whisper the last part. And Mr. James is done pretending, too.

"All right, y'all. Can we move on to the next round?"

We all clap to let him know we're ready.

CHAPTER 18

AFTER MARIA'S PRACTICE MATCH EVERY-body comes over to our house and it's *so loud* in here. It's bad enough when it's just me, Maria, and C.J. crackin' up at each other's jokes but when you add grown-ups, brothers, and sisters? Whoa. Things get wild. In one corner Uncle Jamaal and Uncle Edwin go between sounding like they're arguing about a game and laughing at stuff that used to happen "back in the day." In the kitchen, Dad is floating over all the food on the counter like he was the chef and he's still taking stuff off the grill but everybody knows he ordered it all from Westside

Wings. On the couch, DeShawn and Markus stare at the TV with game controllers in their hands, yelling threats at each other. Moms, Auntie Sharon, and Auntie Julia are sitting around the kitchen table passing their phones to each other. Probably showing off embarrassing pictures of us as usual. Moms is always snapping pictures of us around the house without us knowing. It's no doubt my aunties do it, too. Aaron and Camille keep going in and out of the kitchen for more food when they think nobody's looking. We all know they're the reason the lemon pepper wings disappeared so fast. *I'm onto you, big bro.*

I sit across from Maria in a chair by the window in the front room with two fries sticking out of my mouth from under my top lip. "You know what a walruth thoundth like?" I ask her, tryna get her to smile...or at least say something.

"Have *you* ever heard a walrus before?" she says back, rolling her eyes and pretending she doesn't wanna laugh. We bust out laughing anyway. I don't even wanna know what they sound like. My face gets a little warm finally seeing my best friend laugh for real for the first time since we left the school. While everybody is all over the house, laughing and eating, she's been staring out the window like her cat ran away. She seemed so happy before we left the school. Then something changed. She stops laughing and gets quiet again, and I chew up the fries that were supposed to be fake walrus teeth. "All that work for nothing," she finally says.

"What you mean? Everybody was clapping for you today. And you remember what that Super Nintendo person said?! And did you *see* the looks on their faces that night at the shelter? You were so cool. I could never do that."

"What do *YOU* mean, Simon? I don't know anybody else around here who got skills like you. You made all that stuff up on the spot...and RHYMED IT! I wouldn't be so brave if it wasn't for you," she says, looking up at me. My throat feels dry all of a sudden thinking about Maria being brave because of me. I don't even know how that's possible. I feel so scared *every* time. Ehm—excuse me—I mean, the Notorious D.O.G. don't like a whole bunch of people staring at him and those people he didn't know made him feel a little funny, nah'mean?!

I don't know what to say.

"What y'all over here talkin' 'bout?" C.J. asks, walking up with a plate of lemon pepper wings that he puts on the little table in between all three of us. "Thought they was all gone, didn't you? You know me better than that."

"Maria over here lookin' all sad like she didn't just change the WHOLE WORLD!"

Maria rolls her eyes extra hard.

"Out here actin' like she didn't SHAKE THE WHOLE SCHOOL UP!" C.J. chimes in, even though he still doesn't all the way know what I'm talking about. A smile starts spreading across Maria's face so big, there's no way she can keep being sad about the past week.

OUR FAVORITE GIRL JUST CHANGED THE WORLD!
SHE WENT WILDER THAN WILD UP THERE, LIKE A SQUIRREL
OR A SILLY WALRUS...CAN'T BE SAD AFTER ALL THIS!

LET THAT SMILE OUT! FUN TIMES WHAT YOU CALL
THIS!

EVERYBODY'S HERE JUST VIBIN' AND CHILLIN'.
GOOD FOOD, GOOD FRIENDS, AN AMAZING
FEELIN'.
MOMS OVER THERE LAUGHING, HANGING WITH
HER SISTAS.

I BET YOU SHE'S SHARING SOME EMBARRASSING
PICTURES!

BUT I'LL LET IT SLIDE THIS TIME. (*I LOVE YOU,
MA!*)
DAD'S BY THE FOOD TRYNA GUARD IT,
HA--HA!

EVERYBODY KNOWS WHERE THESE WINGS CAME
FROM
BUT DON'T YOU WORRY, YOU'RE STILL CHEF
NUMBER 1!

AND C.J., MY BOY, COMIN' THROUGH IN THE
CLUTCH,

GOT THEM WINGS ON A PLATE ALL SAVED FOR
US!

THAT'S A REAL TEAMMATE, YOU DA MVP

CUZ YOU KNOW WE LOVE CHICKEN, RI--RI AND
ME!

SEE, AARON AND CAMILLE, THEY BE THINKIN'
THEY SLICK,

GOING IN AND OUT THE KITCHEN ON A WHOLE
BUNCH OF TRIPS.

WE BEEN WATCHING Y'ALL TWO, READIN' YOU
LIKE A BOOK,

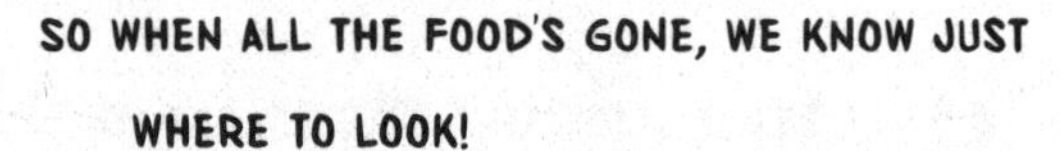

SO WHEN ALL THE FOOD'S GONE, WE KNOW JUST
WHERE TO LOOK!

NOW EVERYBODY'S THINKIN', *WHAT'S HE GON' SAY
NOW?*

I SEE MARKUS AND DESHAWN ON THE COUCH
GETTIN' LOUD.

THEY WAS YELLING, I GUESS CUZ SOMEONE JUST
LOST.

THEY BETTER QUIET DOWN BEFORE MOMS
TURNS IT OFF!

UNCLE J AND UNCLE E TALKING 'BOUT THEY
PAST.

THEY WAS ARGUING AT FIRST, NOW THEY
SHARING A LAUGH.
AUNT SHARON, AUNT JULIA, DOIN' THAT, TOO,
ON EACH OTHER'S PHONES, TALKIN' 'BOUT "LOOK
HOW THEY GREW!"

NOW THAT JUST LEAVES YOU, MARIA, YOU'RE A
STAR.
A REAL ACTIVIST, THAT'S WHO YOU ARE!
AND WHEN YOU NEED SOMEONE TO RAP ON THE
STAGE, THAT'S ME!
CUZ I'M SIMON, THE NOTORIOUS D.O.G.
WOOF WOOF!

This time when the room explodes it isn't so strange. It don't feel so weird to have our families clapping and smiling at me. I'm looking around at everybody's face, hoping Maria sees the same thing I'm seeing: all of us, together feeling happy. That feels pretty special. To me, everything we did this past week worked. Something feels different. And what that person at the school in the suit said gotta mean something.

Maria's family is the last to leave, and before she

walks out the door, she turns around and squeezes me. I don't know what to do, so I just freeze and close my eyes. When she doesn't let go, I hug her back. There's no Bobby or Victor G. around to make fun of me for hugging my best friend.

When everybody's gone, Dad calls me back over to the kitchen sink. You'd think because we did all that work that Dad would let me off the hook! Wrong. He hands me a towel as I step up on the stool next to the counter. "Big week, huh? How you feelin', man? How does it feel to go *viral*?" Dad asks this while rinsing off a cup, then handing it to me.

"Good, I guess."

"Good, *I guess*?"

"I mean, I guess it felt pretty cool for all those people to think I can rap. And, like, I know we did a lot of good things, and all that, and I think Ms. Berry did finally listen to us, but what if Aaron didn't record us? Or Mr. James didn't show the video to her? I lost that whole notebook even after she told me not to and...and..."

"Let it go, Si" is all Dad says for a few minutes as he dunks the last few dishes into the soapy water, rinses, and hands them to me. When the last of the spoons and forks are on the clean side waiting for me to dry them off, Dad turns toward me. "Listen to me: Everybody makes mistakes, son. *Everybody.* Things don't change because we didn't do everything perfectly. Things change because we try."

"But she...but I..."

"Mistakes give us a chance to learn. So if you think about it, son, you don't really make mistakes. You learn new ways to do things so you're better at it next time. Or so you can help somebody else if it happens to them. Did you learn anything this past week?" I stand there thinking about his question for a few seconds.

"That I shouldn't wear so many shirts to school. I'm just gon' have to take 'em off anyway if the AC broke!"

Dad puts his face in his hand and by the way his shoulders start bouncing I know he's laughing at me. *Wrong.*

"Si, I know you can dig deeper than that. What did you learn about what you can *do,* son?" I try to think some more, and it starts to feel like it's taking too long. But then I think I know the answer. It comes out in a whisper. "What's that?" he asks me, leaning in. It's so quiet in the kitchen now that all we hear is the sound of water dripping from the faucet.

"We don't always need flash cards?" I repeat.

"And what do you think *that* means?"

"Um..." Why does this feel like an annoying riddle?!

Dad kneels in front of me. "It means all you ever need is your voice to fight. If it hadn't been for you this weekend, a whole lotta people might have ignored what your friend had to say. You got their attention, Si. You got their attention because you spoke up in a way that only *you* could. Your friend *needed* you, and you were there. You helped her fight even though it wasn't all about you. It don't get much more *notorious* than that. Go on and wash up for bed. I'm proud of you, and you've done more than enough. I'll take it from here."

I start moving quick out of Dad's way and down the hallway before he can change his mind.

"And Simon..." *Dang! Maybe not fast enough.*

"Yeah, Dad?"

"I'ma make a little stop over to the school tomorrow afternoon. I'ma be off and maybe I can take a look at those old air conditioners. See what I can do for y'all. Ain't got but two hands... but I can see." He winks at me and turns back to the sink. Maria and Dad are like the same people. Always handling business!

As I get closer to our room, I hear DeShawn and Markus cheering from inside our room. I push the door open on my way to the bathroom to see what's up, only to find them hovered over Aaron's shoulders, with all three of them looking into the bright light of Aaron's phone. "What y'all doin'?"

Markus answers me by saying, "Come here, bro." I walk over toward Markus's bed and Aaron scoots over to make some space for me. Now all four of us are looking into the bright light of Aaron's phone. Aaron hits Play on the video where they left off. A few seconds later all of us are rocking back and forth to the beat the crowd is clapping to in the video.

WE ALL DESERVE PROGRAMS, CLUBS, AND
  TEAMS
CUZ WE ALL GOT WISHES, HOPES, AND DREAMS.
WE FIGHT FOR OUR RIGHTS, WE THE KIDS WITH
  HEART!

WE JUST ASK THAT YOU JOIN US AND PLAY YOUR
  PART!

SO WHEN I SAY "GIVE US," Y'ALL SAY "THE
  CLUBS!"

GIVE US (THE CLUBS!), GIVE US (THE CLUBS!)
WHEN I SAY "GIVE US," Y'ALL SAY "THE CLUBS!"
GIVE US (THE CLUBS!), GIVE US (THE CLUBS!)

ACKNOWLEDGMENTS

Moms, you're the MVP and you've always been that to me. As kids, we used to hate when you'd take us to the library and we'd stay there for hours, but I guess it paid off, right? Your little boy has a book on shelves that real-life people can choose to buy. Praise Jesus! Would you ever have thought? I'm sure your answer is, "Uh, yeah—cuz you're *my* son." Well, here we are, and it only happened because of you. Thanks for being so gracious with me and loving me even when I didn't see what you saw. Now you can take your grandkids to the library or to the bookstore to check this one out! And you know what? I'll even see if I can get the author to sign it for them—just because I love you. Keep being a trooper. Love, Mookie.

Dionté, your love for reading has always inspired

me. The reason I started reading more is because I once saw you with a book that had hundreds of pages and knew I couldn't let you show me up. So, I went and got two books with hundreds of pages, and the rest is sibling-rivalry history! I'll let you think you're a better reader than me if you promise to take a look at this one in your spare time. Wait—never mind—you'll never be that, but you'll always be my big, little brother! I love you, dude.

DeJhari, you're the best sister I've ever had. To date, lovingly helping raise you alongside Mommy has been one of my greatest accomplishments. I feel honored to be your brother, and to be honest, I think you're one of the biggest reasons why I love kids. I remember when you suggested that we start our own book club. It was such an awesome idea, and hearing you break down literature with such ease was absolutely beautiful. Your mind, your talent, your humor, your thoughtfulness, and your care for others are all tremendous things, and I can't wait to see how you continue to use who you are to help make the world a better place. I love you, Jhari.

Dear Nana and Papa, thank you for being awesome grandparents. Nana, you taught me how to read. 'Nuff said. Game changer. You win. But also, thanks for letting me take all those naps at your house, and for singing "In the Name of Jesus" to me. It was comforting. You have always been my comfort. You're definitely my #1 Nana. And Papa, thank you for helping me to T-H-I-N-K. You've always been so careful and thoughtful with everything, and thankfully, I think those traits have been passed down to me. Thank you for letting me grow up in the house you built. I love you both.

Elizabeth, you are such a G! I know you do this literary agent stuff for a bunch of people, but you've made me feel like I'm your only client. I don't feel like I'm just any random ol' author with you; I feel like THE author with you! You make this feeling happen. Thank you for taking a shot on a kid from Chicago who didn't know nothin' about nothin'. And thank you for always challenging me and fighting for me. You should be proud of your work, EB. Thank you.

Sam, from the moment we spoke together on

the phone that first time, I *knew* I was going to publish with you and Little, Brown. You believed in Simon, and I felt that energy from you immediately. In fact, I literally only chose LBYR because of you. You have been one of the most gracious and sweetest editors during this whole process, and I wish you nothing but success and happiness moving forward. Thank you, Sam.

Ellien, thank you for helping me bring Simon to life! God gives us dreams, but He also places people in our life who He knows will make those dreams come true. You're definitely one of those people for me. Thank you, friend.

Shout-out to all the kids on the West Side of Chicago. Y'all are some of the brightest, funniest, most beautiful people in the entire world. Don't ever let anybody tell you what you can't do. Put on for y'all's city, man. I love you to bits and pieces.

Dear Chaseton and Cambridge, thank you both for changing my everything. You two being here has redeemed so much in my life. I can't wait to see you all reading books like Simon and many others.

Maybe y'all will even rap like your pops one day. Whatever you do, you'll both be great. Daddy loves you so much.

Dear Simoné, a full book couldn't completely capture what I feel for you. I have loved you since we were Simon's age, and I will love you until the last chapter of our life is complete. Thank you for being my everything, Monie. Love, Dwaynie Pooh.

TURN THE PAGE FOR A SNEAK PEEK OF SIMON'S LATEST RHYMING ADVENTURE IN

AVAILABLE APRIL 2023

CHAPTER 1

I LOVE CHICAGO MORE THAN ANYTHING. Low-key, Creighton Park wouldn't be the same anywhere else. Even with the ground covered in snow, like it is today, I know every crack in the sidewalk. I know which places have the best grape pop, which stores to stay away from cuz the owners are mean, and which places have the best Italian beef sandwiches. On a day like today, a sandwich like that—thin-sliced beef, just enough spice, and a bun that's been dipped in hot gravy—would be heaven.

Now, I like the winter, and the snow is pretty and everything, but every now and then we get this thing called the Polar Vortex—a swirling mass of air that comes down from way up north and makes it colder than that thang, with temperatures about ten below and wind chill even colder. On days like today, I wish our school district could be like other cities and let us stay home and watch kids pulling pranks on YouTube. But Chicago hardly ever closes the schools cuz of the weather. My older brother, Aaron, said they closed once when the snow was up to his butt, but I never got a snow day. If the snow was up to *my* butt, I'd have to trudge through it. School would be open, and there would be Mr. James, jumping on his desk to do a rap about barometric pressure or something.

It'd probably be a good rap, too. Even the Notorious D.O.G. gotta admit Mr. James got skills.

But the WORST part is we're stuck inside for recess. Which makes no sense. Sometimes the heaters don't work right, so today it's just as cold inside as outside. Maria worked hard to get us stuff like the schools on the North Side have, but I guess they ain't got around to the radiators at Booker T. Washington yet. All I know is that Polar Vortex mess ought to stay up in the North Pole, where it belong, and let us keep having recess outside, where *it* belongs.

It's the sixth straight day we have to stay inside, and nobody is happy. But I'm lookin' on the bright side: At least all the recess equipment is in here.

"Hey, fellas, I got the ball!" Maria spins the red kickball on her fingertip. She only just learned to do it, so she shows it off every chance she gets. I guess that's one good thing about having recess in the gym: no freezing-cold wind to blow the ball off her finger.

"Cool," I tell her. "You wanna go play wall ball over there?"

"We should change it up and shoot some hoops," says C.J.

Or, I think that's what he says. It's loud in the gym. In one corner a bunch of girls are jumping up and down and screaming cheers. In another, a bunch of people from Mrs. Leary's class play dodge-ball with Nerf balls, only they can't keep track of who's actually playing, and who's just getting too close, so a whole bunch of people are just getting hit. Out of the game before they even start playing!

"I'm not sure we can play hoops *or* wall ball," I say, looking around the gym. "All the walls and hoops already being used!"

"Then let's just toss it around," says Maria. She throws it at me, but I don't move fast enough. It goes right over my head, *whoosh*, and right into Bobby Sanchez's palm.

"You need to throw it way lower to get on Simon's level." Bobby smirks at me. Will he ever come up with new material? I'm short. We KNOW. He ain't gotta bring it up every single day.

He throws the ball and it whizzes over my head going the other way. C.J. tries to grab it but Victor G., Bobby's main sidekick, shoves into him and makes him drop it. "This is mine, loser." Then Victor shoots, and the ball goes straight through the metal hoop nearby, right in the middle of somebody's game of Horse.

I might've been impressed if he didn't turn and look at me all smug.

I wish I didn't have to deal with Bobby and Victor *still* clowning on me all the time. I might be short on the outside, but the Notorious D.O.G. is big on the inside. One of these days Bobby and Victor are gon' put some respect on my name.

IF IT'S H...O...R--S--E
PLAYIN' WALL BALL OR SHOOTIN' REAL LONG THREES

AROUND BOBBY SANCHEZ OR VICTOR G.
OR ANYBODY ELSE--THEY GON' NOTICE ME!
I'M SIMON THE BALLER, SIMON THE GOAT
SIMON, THE BEST ON THE COURT (I HOPE)
WELL, MAYBE NOT THE BEST, BUT I'M STILL IN THE GAME
SO WHATEVER Y'ALL DO, JUST RESPECT MY NAME!

Someone throws the ball back, and C.J snatches it before Victor can grab it. I run a few feet over, so this time when C.J. passes it to me I can get it. Then I turn and get in position to shoot a three-pointer. I'm wide open!

Except the hoop is looking real far away right now.

I hold up a second, and when I do, Bobby starts in.

"Bet you can't make that," he says.

He's probably right. We're back behind the three-point line, and anyway, I'm not exactly dressed for sports right now. Since it's so cold outside, Moms was all into me this morning about wearing layers. So I got on my Bulls T-shirt, the Bulls hoodie I got for Christmas, jeans, and long underwear. I didn't want to wear those long johns because that's just embarrassing, but when that wind cut through all them layers this morning, I was glad Moms made me put them on.

But now I'm standing here sweatin' in all these layers.

"Bet you he can," says C.J.

Now I'm in for it.

"Okay," says Bobby. "Let's make this interesting and bet for real."

Now I'm *really* in for it. Sometimes we tell C.J. he should speak up more, but look what happens when he does!

"I just know y'all ain't gambling," drops in Maria.

"We ain't gamblin' with money," C.J. says to her. "We gamblin' with snacks! You got a bag of Flamin' Hots for lunch?"

Bobby nods and grins. "Two of 'em."

"Aight, then. Bet."

"You're on."

Maria pushes her glasses—blue frames today—up on her nose. "That's still probably against the rules. And anyway, people are using that hoop."

"We all gotta share when we're doing indoor recess," says C.J. I can already see him getting excited about two free bags of Flamin' Hot Cheetos. I don't want to let him down, or look like a fool in front of Bobby.

But I'm *really* not feelin' this three-point-line nonsense.

"I'm not sure, y'all," I say. It's hard to shoot wearing long johns.

"What are you scared of, shorty?" Bobby again. Can't he go somewhere else? Anywhere else?

Then Victor starts in. "SHORTY SIMON IS A CHICKEN! *BAWK-BOK!*"

I can see Maria getting ready to say something but I shake my head. "Ignore him!"

"WE ALL KNOW SIMON'S GONNA LOSE CUZ CHICKENS CAN'T PLAY BASKETBALL!" Victor yells, hands cupped around his mouth.

"BAWK-BOK!"

"Ain't no chickens over here!" Notorious D.O.G. ain't never scared! *Well, maybe just a little bit.*

"If Simon is the chicken, why you the one doin' all the cluckin'?" Maria is all in Bobby's face, which is turning all kinds of red. He hates when people come at him like that.

BOBBY THINKS HE'S SO TOUGH STUFF
ALL HE DOES IS HUFF AND PUFF
I WISH I WAS BRAVE ENOUGH
TO TELL HIM TO HIS FACE, "ENOUGH!"
EVERYBODY'S WATCHING US
SO EVERY WORD IS GETTING STUCK

WON'T COME OUT, WON'T COME UP
ALL OF THIS IS JUST TOO MUCH!
THEY SAYIN' THAT I'M SCARED--YUP!
CHICKEN SIMON, CLUCK CLUCK!

I JUST NEED A LITTLE LUCK
TO MAKE THE SHOT I'M 'BOUT TO CHUCK!

C.J. leans in. "You got this. And I'll get you Flamin' Hots, too, after school."

It's now or never. And if it's never I won't ever

live it down. Then nobody will ever respect the Notorious D.O.G.

I close my eyes real tight and let go.

Feels like a million minutes till I hear it.

Swish!

Then: "OH EM GEE, SIMON!"

No way I made that. No way. But I did!

People are cheering like I just made the winning shot in sudden-death overtime. And C.J. is shaking my hand, all official and dramatic. "You just won yourself a bag of Flamin' Hots!"

Michael Hicks

DWAYNE REED is America's favorite rapping teacher from Chicago and the author of *Simon B. Rhymin'*. He is known for his viral music videos and hit songs, "Welcome to the 4th Grade" and "Welcome to Kindergarten." When he's not writing, rapping, or teaching, Dwayne can be found presenting at educator conferences across the US, or loving on his beautiful wife, Simoné, and their children, Chase and Cambridge. He invites you to follow him on Twitter and Instagram @TeachMrReed.